Whispers of the Past

Ceridwen Hughson

L Y C A N
B O O K S

Myrddin Publishing
unique electronic & print books

Contents

CERIDWEN HUGHSON

Foreword

Whispers of the Past is set in my hometown of Aberystwyth in Wales. This means there are some Welsh words and phrases sprinkled throughout that I thought I should mention. Here are some commonly used ones to know:

- Bore da - Good morning (pronounced "Bore-e dah")
- Cariad - A term of endearment, like "love" or "sweetheart"
- Ceredigion - The county where Aberystwyth is located
- Cwtch - A hug or cuddle
- Diolch - Thank you
- Ffion - Pronounced "Fee-on," a popular Welsh name
- Ffion's Ffwrn - Ffion's Oven, the name of her bakery
- Hwyl - Goodbye
- Fach - Little (used as an affectionate term in this novel, pronounced "Va-ch," The ch is like the Scottish Loch)
- Mam - Mom/mum
- Moron - Carrot
- Nain – Grandmother (pronounced "Nine")
- Prynhawn da - Good afternoon (pronounced "prun-hown dah")
- Ych a fi - Yuk
- Yr Wylan Fach – The Small Seagull, a made-up pub in this book.
- And as you pronounce "c" with a hard sound in Welsh, my name is K-eridwen Hewson, (I had to get that in here)

Along with some Celtic names, the rest is written in British English. I hope you enjoy this glimpse into Wales's unique words and culture as you turn the pages.

Chapter 1

Eleri stepped out of her battered campervan onto the familiar street. She locked the door securely, patting the beleaguered paintwork with affection. The van was crammed floor to ceiling with the remnants of her previous life, teetering stacks of books, overflowing bags of clothing, and a dubious collection of tea towels with animal memes. A chill spring breeze wound its way through the narrow lanes of Aberystwyth, bringing with it memories of her childhood. She pulled her coat tighter as her eyes landed on the faded blue door of her aunt's bakery.

Eleri's gaze returned to the campervan for a moment, parked along the curb. For a blink, the vehicle warped before her eyes. Metal groaning, glass shattering, the camper twisted into an unrecognisable tangle of debris.

Eleri jerked back; eyes wide. She blinked rapidly until the destroyed vehicle reformed back into its former state. Just a flicker, a trick of the shadows and tired eyes after her long journey from London.

With a dismissive gesture of her head, Eleri turned away. She rubbed her temples, blaming the strange vision on one too many hours behind the wheel. Nothing but exhaustion fogging her mind and eyes. Her mind's way of dealing with the car crash of her life she left behind. With a shake of her head, she composed herself. She walked up to the door, turning the worn brass knob, hesitating before turning it. As the door swung open, morning light glinted off the cracked, gold lettering that adorned the glass pane. Eleri stepped closer to admire the elegant script that spelled out "Knead a Cwtch Bakery."

The bell jingled overhead, announcing her arrival into the empty shop. Dust motes swirled in the weak sunlight filtering through the large front windows. The smell of neglect and decay welcomed her. Eleri's shoulders slumped as she took in the dusty bakery interior. Her stomach twisted in knots. Was she up to this?

Eleri ran her fingers over the wooden countertops, remembering helping her aunt out in the holidays.

Tilting her head with a wistful shake, she made her way behind the counter and through the swinging door into the kitchen. Shelves lined the walls, stocked with jars of spices and empty tubs of flour and sugar. Dusty pots and baking sheets hung from the ceiling. Cobwebs draped from the pots and pans, intricate patterns of dusty webs tangled together.

At the heart of the room stood the giant commercial mixer Ffion had nicknamed Ol' Bessie. It brought back memories of her aunt covered in flour, cheerfully kneading bread dough and sharing funny customer stories.

Eleri sighed, feeling the weight of her aunt's absence. This kitchen had been Ffion's pride and joy. She had poured her heart into this bakery for over thirty years. And now it was Eleri's turn, along with all the memories it held.

She may as well see what else was in store. The creaking stairs protested her steps as she climbed up to the flat above the shop. Her fingers traced the smooth wooden banister, polished by decades of use.

She paused on the landing, gazing at the photos lining the wall. There she was as a chubby-cheeked three-year-old, proudly holding a sponge cake with more icing on her than the cake. Another at seven in her netball uniform, missing front teeth displayed in a wide grin.

Eleri moved into the sunny, familiar kitchen. The floral wallpaper seemed more faded than she remembered, but the cheerful blue cabinets still exuded home. She patted the Formica table, picturing her younger self colouring while Ffion bustled around cooking.

After her parents had died, Ffion had become so much more

than an aunt. She had provided stability and comfort when Eleri's world shattered.

The flat was bringing back memories long forgotten. She smiled faintly, recalling the pale morning light filtering through lace curtains as they prepared the day's baking. Fiona's sleeves would be rolled up, her red hair trapped in a pink hairnet, flowery and frilly apron dusted with flour and spices. The apron was a joke Christmas present, the last gift under the tree one year. It had taken weeks of scouring Aber for the kitschiest item she could find. She'd loved it and even insisted on wearing it in front of customers, enjoying Eleri's acute embarrassment. Ffion was fearless.

She remembered her younger self perched at the kitchen table, listening to Aunt Ffion's warm laughter. Eleri could almost taste the sweet chamomile tea that would lazily steep while she urged just one more story before bed.

Later, snuggled under piles of quilts upstairs, the old house would creak and settle around her. Eleri always felt cradled in those moments - by the building, by her memories, by Ffion's love. Her aunt was the closest thing to a mother she'd known after losing her parents.

Those memories of becoming a family with Ffion enveloped Eleri. She owed her aunt so much - those years had given her a sense of home she hadn't even realised she was missing. Ffion's loving companionship had carried her through grief.

Eleri blinked, the present-day kitchen coming back into focus. Eleri glanced at the bouquet of dried flowers hanging by the window. Daisies had been Ffion's favourite. Plucking out a few loose flowers, Eleri headed down the hall to her childhood bedroom.

The white door revealed her room just as she remembered. Pale blue walls decorated with posters of boy bands and animals. A white pine bed tucked under the sloped ceiling. Her stuffed animals arranged against the pillows, waiting for her to come back. How many times had her poor aunt bumped her head on the sloped rafters over the years? Probably too many to count. Eleri smiled at the memory. Ffion never complained though, laughing it off whenever she misjudged the height. Probably explained why Eleri got the bigger room, though.

With a bittersweet mix of grief and nostalgia, Eleri placed the daisies on her pillow. She sat on the side of the bed and picked up Ducky, the stuffed duck. Tracing the frayed edges of his bright yellow bill, she allowed the memories to wash over her.

Saturday mornings helping in the bakery, sneaking out hot sausage rolls when Ffion wasn't looking. Long bike rides with Mary and Seren along the seaside cliffs with the freezing wind whipping through her hair. Curled up on this very bed on rainy days, reading while wrapped in her favourite fuzzy blanket.

She glanced around at the relics of her youth. Posters, books, trinkets, all pieces of who she once was. This was before life's complications and responsibilities weighed her down. Back when she thought anything was possible.

Setting Ducky aside, Eleri stood abruptly. The past was gone, no matter how warmly she looked back on it. She was here to sort out Ffion's affairs and decide the fate of the bakery, not linger in nostalgia.

Eleri left her bedroom and entered Ffion's across the hall. She spun, taking it all in. The patchwork quilt, crafted over years. Lace curtains filtering the afternoon light. A vase of dried flowers on the dresser, daisies, of course, a small smile twitched her lips, and lavender.

Opening the wooden wardrobe released a waft of her aunt's perfume. Eleri pressed her face into one of Ffion's soft cardigans, breathing deeply. It still smelled like her.

Eleri sank down on the edge of the bed, throat tight. She picked up the framed photo on the nightstand. A young Ffion beamed up at her, arm slung around her best friend - Eleri's mother.

Tears pricked Eleri's eyes, a knot tightening in her throat. She missed them both so terribly. The ache of their loss was as raw as the day they had passed.

But she had been given so much in the years she'd had with

them, she reminded herself. Joy-filled memories she'd have forever.

Eleri set the photo down, swiping the tears from her cheeks. She wasn't going to wallow in sadness. Not when there was so much still ahead.

Standing, Eleri left the bedroom with renewed focus. Sentimentality served no purpose right now, she reminded herself. She strode to the spare room that served as Ffion's office, careful to avoid anything that could set off anymore memories.

The room was the smallest in the building. Its walls lined with folders on one side and books on the other with only a small window facing the garden for natural light. Eleri sat at the desk and opened the bakery accounts ledger. Ffion didn't believe in computers.

"I have an accountant for that sort of thing," she'd said. As Eleri scanned the neat numbers, the slight hint of voices began whispering at the edges of her mind. Barely there, but unmistakable. A chill crawled down her spine.

She shook her head. Not now! She dismissed it as nerves and grief playing tricks. She shook the page she was looking at and bent closer.

The ledger page blurred as the whispers grew louder, more insistent. Eleri dropped her head into her hands with a groan. Why now, after all these years?

Panic rising, she clamped her eyes shut, clapping her hands over her ears, desperately trying to block it out. But the voices pushed through the mental barrier, like mist rolling from the sea.

Eleri shuddered as ghostly words surrounded her. She couldn't work out what they were saying. She never could. They became deafening, unrelenting. Her chair screeched on the hardwood floor as she pushed away from the desk. She had to get out of there.

Eleri burst through the bakery's back door into the garden, sucking in fresh air like a fish gasping for water. She leaned against the cold brick wall, breathing hard. The whispers faded until all she could hear were cars interspersed with seagull cries and her heart hammering inside her ribs.

For years, she had suppressed her ability to sense spirits. She hadn't missed it – the fear, the lack of privacy, the bone-chilling voices. Why was it back now?

Chapter 2

Composing herself, Eleri sauntered down the winding lane towards the seafront. She needed a distraction, she decided. As she walked, memories surfaced of this same route to visit her friend Seren's bookshop.

The familiar sight snatched Eleri's breath as she turned the corner. There stood the quaint bookshop, looking almost frozen in time. Its display window still boasted a jumble of leather-bound volumes and framed prints. The gilt lettering over the door gleamed despite the years, spelling out 'Aber Books' in elegant script on the swinging wooden sign.

Next door, the antique shop's dark wooden facade and glass doors tugged at her memory just the same. Gareth's father had run it back then, but she guessed it now belonged to Gareth. The stores had always existed side by side, one feeding the locals' thirst for adventures on the page, the other for relics of the past.

Heart fluttering, Eleri approached the door. She and Gareth had been close during her teens. He was almost a year older, mature, and seemed worldly to her inexperienced eyes, always there in the background – a genuine friend. They had drifted apart after Eleri moved away with John to university. She shook her head. Stop thinking about John, she reprimanded herself. Eleri brushed her hands through her long auburn waves. She was here to forget John, not dwell on him. She heard through the grapevine that Gareth had married shortly after she left to an incomer from Birmingham, a librarian up at the National Library. It had only lasted a couple of years.

Through the window, Eleri glimpsed a dark-haired man arranging items. He was dressed in a casual button-down shirt, sleeves rolled up to reveal tanned, muscular forearms.

Faded jeans hugged his legs in all the right places.

Eleri's palms grew sweaty as she approached the door. She ran a shaky hand through her hair, this time tucking the unruly strands behind her ears. Her heart pounded against her ribs—why was she so nervous? With a bracing breath, she stepped inside.

A charming clutter greeted her - furniture, artwork, and knickknacks from various eras. The man turned at the sound of the door. Wide shoulders and a strong stubbled jaw came into view as recognition flashed in his warm brown eyes.

"Eleri?" Gareth's eyes widened in surprise, taking her in.

She rubbed a hand self-consciously over the wrinkles in her shirt, regretting not changing after the long drive.

"It's me," she said with an awkward wave, nerves making her voice croak. His handsome face broke into an easy grin.

"I can't believe it. Look at you, all grown up!"

Eleri's pulse quickened. "It's been a while."

An uncomfortable silence descended. Eleri pretended to examine a nearby jewellery box.

"I, er, heard about your aunt," Gareth finally offered. "I'm sorry."

Eleri nodded, throat tightening. "It's just me now." She attempted a casual shrug.

"Sorry about, you know, your wife."

Gareth's face fell and Eleri could have kicked herself for mentioning it.

"You're back to stay?" He asked.

"I think so. The bakery is mine now, so..." Eleri trailed off with another half-hearted shrug. She was acutely aware of Gareth studying her face.

"Well, it's great to have you back in Aber," he said.

Eleri's gaze darted up to find him studying her with knowing eyes. She grimaced and turned away, arms folded over her chest.

"I should get going, but let's catch up soon, yeah?" She offered him a fleeting smile before hurrying out of the shop.

Safely outside, Eleri sucked in deep breaths. Gareth had dredged up memories and feelings she thought were long buried. He hadn't been interested then. Why would he be now? They had completely different lives. And she had a bakery to run. Eleri pushed aside thoughts of the past. Eleri made her way back through the snaking lanes, all thoughts of visiting the bookshop forgotten.

The next few days passed in a blur of attending to bakery affairs. Eleri cleaned, tidied, and sorted paperwork. Keeping busy kept her mind off Gareth and the persistent spirit whispers.

One late afternoon, the sun slanted through the bakery windows as Eleri scrubbed years of grime from the glass display cases. She focused on banishing every last streak, trying to ignore the whispery echoes that drifted around her. They were too faint to make out, yet they were getting louder; something about those wispy voices chilled her blood.

A sudden loud bang shattered the silence. Eleri gasped and whirled around, heart lurching. Gareth stood frozen by the entrance, the closing door still quivering from the force of his entry.

"Gareth!" Eleri pressed a hand to her chest as relief flooded through her. The voices evaporated like mist. She let out a shaky laugh, scolding herself for being so easily spooked. It was just her imagination playing tricks, conjuring phantom voices from old memories that still lingered here. There was no such thing as ghosts, she reminded herself.

"You, OK?" he asked, eyebrows raised.

"Yes! Sorry, you startled me," Eleri said with an embarrassed laugh.

Gareth glanced around the empty bakery. "Got a minute to catch up?"

Eleri nodded. She followed him to a small table by the window. As they talked about old memories and recent developments, the whispers faded away to nothing.

"So, what happened with you and your wife?" Eleri asked, her voice cautious. "I heard you got divorced a few years ago."

Gareth's expression darkened briefly. "Yeah, it just didn't work out, unfortunately. She hated it here, wanted the excitement of the city." He sighed. "What about you? I know you went off to university with that boyfriend of yours."

Eleri nodded, looking down at the table. "John. We're not together anymore." She shook her head. "John wanted me to get some boring office job to support us," Eleri said with a sigh. "Meanwhile, he did nothing but focus on his own career."

She shook her head. "At home, it was even worse. He sat around while I cleaned, cooked, did all the household jobs. Like I was his unpaid skivvy."

Gareth's forehead creased in a frown. "You deserved so much better than that. You had dreams of your own."

"He laughed at my baking, even though he gobbled up pretty much everything I made." Eleri's voice grew quiet. "Said it wasn't a real career."

She met Gareth's sympathetic brown eyes. "With him, I was more like a housekeeper that he took for granted than an actual partner."

"That's awful," Gareth replied, brow furrowing. "You always loved cooking. You were always helping out your aunt here." His arms swept out.

"I did," Eleri said wistfully. "I felt stifled with him. Like I was a different person, a shadow of myself." She pulled strands of her auburn hair forward, curling them with her fingers. "Coming back here, it feels like coming home. Being free to start over. You know?"

"Well, for what it's worth, I think you're incredibly brave," Gareth said. "I'm glad you're following your dreams again. You deserve it."

Eleri's cheeks flushed at the unexpected praise. She shyly tucked the lock of hair behind her ear. "It's scary, but also exciting. We'll see where it leads."

She looked into his chocolate-brown eyes. Aber may be sleepy, but at least she felt herself here. With John, she just felt drained. "Now here I am, back where I started," she finished with a self-conscious laugh. "I'm sorry to burden you with all that. You're the first person I've had to talk to since I got back. Unless you count Megan down the shop."

"Oof, maybe not. Tell that girl anything and it'll be twice around Aber before you leave the shop!" They grinned at each other.

Gareth's brown eyes crinkled. "Well, I should head out." He stood up to leave. Give me a heads up if there is anything else you might need, alright?

As Gareth left, Eleri sagged against the table, the day's events suddenly overwhelming. She drew a long, calming breath as the room swam around her.

With her eyes closed, she focused on stilling her scattered thoughts. Gareth had a way of soothing her rattled nerves, that she'd nearly forgotten. He spoke with her so openly, so attentively, as if he truly saw the real Eleri behind the facade.

She hadn't expected to feel such an easy connection after so many years apart. But something in his compassionate, familiar presence made her anxieties recede.

Eleri opened her eyes, feeling centred once more. Perhaps revisiting the past held unexpected rewards. She had underestimated how much she missed Gareth's company.

The next day, Eleri was sorting out cupboards on her hands and knees when she heard the bell jingle. She lifted her head and caught sight of Gareth waving a paper bag.

"Thought you could use a lunch break," he said, holding up the bag. "Fish and chips, just like old times."

Eleri smiled, touched by the gesture. As they ate, laughter came easily. The eight intervening years seemed to melt away. It felt comfortable, familiar - like coming home.

When Gareth left with a promise to stop by soon, Eleri realised with a flutter of nervous excitement that she couldn't wait to see him again.

✳✳✳

Armed with a broom, hair tied back and wearing her aunt's famous apron, Eleri stood in the centre of the bakery and turned, taking it all in. Dust coated every surface, the glass displays were still smudged, and cobwebs clung to the light fixtures. The checkerboard tile floor wrapping around the counter was dull and grimy. She bit her lip.

Gareth was right - restoring the bakery was an enormous undertaking. She wanted to carry on Ffion's legacy, but this went deeper than nostalgia. Eleri needed to prove to herself that she could build something that was hers. For too long she had drifted without purpose, letting life sweep her along. Now she wanted to reshape her future with her own two hands.

The bakery would become the foundation of the new life. Failure was not an option - she had to see this through for both her aunt's memory and for her own sake. She was going to bring the bakery back to its former glory if it killed her.

Tying a bandana over her hair, Eleri turned up the stereo Ffion always played while baking. She sang at the top of her voice along to the upbeat classic hits as she vigorously swept floors and scrubbed down walls and windows. Dirt and grime gradually disappeared, revealing shining surfaces underneath.

Eleri stood back, admiring her progress so far. The main bakery area already looked brighter and cleaner. Now on to the kitchen.

The door creaked open, begging for the hinges to be oiled, and her steps faltered. The kitchen was even grubbier than the front. A fine layer of dust coated every surface. Cobwebs draped from the ceiling and framed the windows. Mouse droppings littered the tiled floor.

With a sigh, Eleri squeezed lemon-scented cleaner onto a cloth, scrubbing the ancient microwave; the squeak of the rubber gloves adding a counterpoint to the music on the radio. A bit of hard work didn't kill anyone, she told herself. Yeah, but she was going to ache tomorrow. Slowly, she worked her way around the room - wiping, sweeping, polishing. Muscles aching, she finally slumped against the central worktable.

A decent dent made, but so much left to do. How had Ffion maintained this place alone for so long? Eleri's stamina clearly needed work.

The next day Eleri returned downstairs, armed with

reinforcements - cleaning supplies and this time, a flask of coffee, so she wouldn't have to stop to make drinks so often. 80s pop blasted once again as she dived into scrubbing flour and batter splatter off the walls around the industrial mixer.

Eleri smiled as she uncovered the baby blue paint underneath. In her mind, she could see Ffion bustling around, singing along to the radio before the sun even rose.

Eleri moved on to the storage shelves lining the walls. She organised jars ready to be filled with spices, and binned boxes of baking powder, and various food colourings.

Reaching way in back, her hand landed on a heavy plastic tub. Sliding it forward revealed a layer of dust so thick she had to wipe a porthole to peer inside.

Squinting through the small opening, Eleri made out stacks of paper. She lugged the storage box off the shelf and onto the central table, coughing at the resulting plume of dust.

Brushing the grime away revealed the words 'Ffion's Recipes' scribbled on the lid in her aunt's looping script. Eleri's heart leapt. She lifted off the lid to find piles of notebooks, loose papers, and faded recipe cards neatly stacked inside.

With hands trembling in anticipation, Eleri lifted out a spiral notebook. Flipping through revealed page after page filled with recipes written in Ffion's neat hand. Breads, cakes, biscuits - going back decades. This was a treasure trove!

Eleri reverently set aside the notebook and picked up a recipe card. Ffion's famous cinnamon rolls. She vividly remembered helping roll the dough, stealing icing.

Next, Eleri pulled out a sheet in Ffion's hurried scrawl - a recipe experiment for lemon tarts. Eleri touched the smeared, blotchy ink where floury hands had handled the paper while cooking.

Each item she withdrew sparked memories - the crunch of shortbread, the tang of lemon drizzle cake, warmth of bara brith. Ffion's life work was here.

Eleri eventually looked up, cheeks stiff with dried tears she hadn't realised she'd shed. Surrounded by Ffion's recipes, she had lost track of time. She began packing the books and cards back in order.

As she worked, Eleri plotted out ideas. The bakery would reopen with Ffion's classics - cinnamon rolls, bara brith, the rich chocolate cakes. Maybe she'd even come up with her own stuff.

Eleri stored the tub on a clean shelf with a satisfied smile. The kitchen was finally shaping up after days of cleaning. She glanced out the window and was surprised to see the sun hanging low in the sky, washing the shop front in golden light. The rumbling in her stomach was becoming too loud to ignore. She pressed a hand to her belly and winced as it let out an audible gurgle.

"You've got to eat something," she murmured to herself. It had been a busy day of organising and tidying, and she realised now that she had completely skipped lunch.

After a quick bite, Eleri wandered the front of the bakery. It still needed a deep clean, but already felt more inviting. It just needed freshly painted walls and to finish cleaning the display cases.

She unlocked the front door, opening it wide. Eleri leaned on the broom handle and watched people strolling by on the pavement. The tantalising scents of nearby restaurants mingled with the sea air. Lights twinkled to life in shop windows as dusk fell over the town.

Eleri imagined her aunt standing in the doorway decades ago, her newly opened bakery awaiting its first customers. Did Ffion feel the same blend of nerves and excitement? Likely even more - she had taken a huge risk branching out on her own. At least she didn't have a mortgage like her aunt had.

Eleri had an immense admiration for her aunt's courage and achievement. Because of her hard work, she carried the benefit of Ffion's reputation and loyal local customer base. All she had to do was follow in her aunt's footsteps.

The broom handle clattered as Eleri set it aside and reached below the bakery counter. She rifled through the stack of brightly coloured flyers, announcing the grand reopening. She should start small, with a soft opening. That would be wise, but if she intended to make a go of it, a splashy celebration was in order. She'd only been here a few weeks, but the money inherited from Ffion would not last long unless she made a success of of it.

Flyers in hand, Eleri slipped out the front door, turning the key in the lock behind her one-handed. She strode purposefully through the winding lanes, taping up flyers as she went. Empty shop fronts and lampposts soon sported cheery announcements fluttering in the breeze.

Reaching the seaside promenade, Eleri took a break, watching the tiny boats bob on the horizon. Satisfied with her work, Eleri headed back to the bakery as the sun dipped low over the harbour. The lamps flickered brighter, as if fuelled by the light of Ffion's approval.

"Thank you, Aunt," Eleri whispered, warmed by the imagined praise. She flipped the sign to "Closed" and got ready to prepare for another busy day.

***

The next morning, Eleri surveyed the pastry display units, mentally calculating dimensions. The massive oak units had been repainted a clean white and polished to a gleam. Now to fill them.

Donning one of Ffion's more demure aprons, Eleri got to work mixing, rolling, and filling using her aunt's tried-and-true recipes. Childhood memories guided her hands - pinch the cinnamon roll dough just so, avoid overmixing the ginger biscuits.

Soon, several trays of cakes and biscuits cooled on every surface. Eleri stepped back, critically eyeing her creations. The cinnamon buns looked a bit wonky, the scones over-browned on one side. But the rich scents made her stomach growl.

For a moment, she saw Ffion fussing over the arrangements, always striving for the perfect display. Eleri may have lacked her aunt's refined eye, but she had paid attention over the years. She grouped items for pleasing heights and pops of colour. Soon, the gleaming cases were filled.

Eleri brewed coffee as the morning sun broke over the ocean. Unlocking the door, she stepped outside. A few early risers were out walking dogs and fetching newspapers.

"Bore da!" she called out.

"Good morning to you too!" returned one lady as she pulled a reluctant dachshund behind her.

Several smiled and waved, a few chatted about her aunt and welcomed Eleri home. She was home.

Back inside, Eleri triple-checked everything was ready. The kitchen prepped, pastries temptingly displayed, coffee brewing. She had even queued up Ffion's favourite upbeat playlist.

With a deep breath, Eleri walked to the front door. She pictured her aunt's smiling face as she flipped the sign to "Open." Before turning back to the counter.

The bell above the door chimed as a plump woman with blond hair tied back in a practical ponytail entered the bakery. Her face lit up when she saw Eleri behind the counter.

"Eleri!" she cried, rushing over to wrap her in an enthusiastic hug. "It's so wonderful to see you back home!"

Eleri laughed, returning the hug. "Great to see you too, Mary."

Mary pulled back, grasping Eleri's hands as her bright blue gaze roved around the shop's interior. "Just look at this place! It's like stepping back in time."

Mary spun, taking in the freshly painted mint walls, gleaming display cases, and polished oak furnishings.

"I can't believe how great it looks," Mary continued. "You've been working magic - I can feel Ffion's spirit in here again."

Eleri smiled, warmed by her friend's praise. "Thanks. It's been a labour of love. I don't want to let her memory down."

"Well, it's charming. I bet she'd be so proud." Mary gave Eleri's hands an affectionate squeeze.

Eleri hoped her friend was right.

"Hopefully, I won't mess up what she started! Can I tempt

you with something?" Eleri offered. "I've been working my way through Ffion's old recipes."

"Ooh, twist my arm, why don't you?" Mary winked. "I'll take a cinnamon bun, please. No one made them like your aunt."

Eleri placed one of the still-warm buns on a plate, inhaling the cinnamon aroma. She and Mary took seats at a table by the window.

"Mmm, that's the stuff," Mary mumbled through a mouthful. "Delicious!"

Eleri smiled. "Remember coming here as kids? Helping Ffion decorate biscuits?"

Mary's eyes took on a nostalgic gleam. "Those are some of my favourite childhood memories. We thought we were so clever, didn't we?"

Chuckling, Eleri sipped her tea. "I seem to recall you eating half the decorations before they made it onto the biscuits."

"Hey now, quality control is a very important job!" Mary protested with a grin. They both dissolved into giggles.

Eleri's heart jumped with affection. She and Mary went all the way back to the first year of secondary school. While Eleri had drifted away over the years, her lively friend still felt familiar as family.

"What about the summer Ffion tried to teach us to make pies?" Eleri asked. "Her technique for weaving the lattice crust was ... difficult."

Mary groaned. "Ugh, I could never get it right! My dough always ripped." She shook her head ruefully. "Meanwhile, you had the perfect lattice every time. Ffion said you were a natural."

"Beginner's luck, I'm sure," Eleri said.

"I still can't cook to save my life," Mary said. "How about you give me a lesson one of these days? For old time's sake?"

"I'd love that." Eleri smiled. "It's nice to talk about Ffion. Keep her memory close, you know?"

Mary's voice was soft with empathy. "Of course. She was important to me, too. We'll keep sharing all the happy memories."

Eleri nodded gratefully. It was so good to see her friend again. Chatting by FriendFace just wasn't the same.

The two talked late into the afternoon until Mary had to rush off. As the door swung shut behind her, the bakery felt very quiet and empty. Eleri busied herself tidying up.

She was collecting crumb-scattered dishes when a cold tingle danced down her spine. The subtle scent of lilacs wafted by. Ffion's favourite perfume. Eleri froze, pulses pounding.

"Ffion?" she whispered. "Is that you?"

Only silence answered. But the flicker of her aunt's presence lingered like the last notes of a favourite song.

Did her aunt ever imagine her life's work would one day pass to Eleri? Her personality was so huge everyone thought she'd live forever. She wished she could ask for Ffion's guidance now. She'd always wanted to run her own business, but now she was doing it, the task seemed herculean.

Locking the front door, Eleri wandered into the kitchen. She trailed her fingers over countertops where her aunt had worked so hard.

Pausing by the cookbooks, her gaze landed on a stained recipe card peeking out. Eleri slid it free and felt a pinch in her heart. "Ffion's Famous Bara Brith" in her aunt's elegant cursive. She did like to toot her old horn sometimes. Then she laughed. If she didn't, who would?

Eleri cradled the fragile card. She could almost see a seven-year-old version of herself sitting on a flour-dusted stool, sticking out her tongue in concentration while mixing the ingredients.

On impulse, she collected the needed ingredients and got to work. Soon the tea was chilling with the fruit soaking in it. Eleri brushed off her hands, overcome with nostalgia.

Eleri prepared a baking sheet and oven on autopilot, lost in memories. She may as well practice making something while she was at it. She stared into thin air for a moment, then smiled. Welsh cakes! For some reason Aunt Ffion didn't make those, so it would be hers. And what weirdo didn't like Welsh cakes? She sprinkled flour and rolled out the dough. Using Ffion's colourful cookie cutters, she pressed out perfect shapes. Who said Welsh cakes had to be round anyway?

She paused. She'd only had one customer today, but tomorrow would be better and you couldn't attract customers with an empty shop! Also, practice makes perfect, she reminded herself.

Eleri turned the stove knob with a soft click, warming the old cast iron pan. She hummed an aimless tune as she waited, using the time to gather ingredients. Measuring and mixing were second nature, each step etched into muscle memory from years at her aunt's side.

Soon the kitchen filled with the scent of baking batter. Eleri smiled as she gently flipped the cakes midway, watching their edges turn golden brown. When they finished, she carefully removed each shape - stars, ovals, rounds - their sweet aroma transporting her through time.

Closing her eyes, she could almost imagine her aunt standing beside her, ready to dust the cakes with powdered sugar. Some nostalgia was best served warm, straight from the pan.

Eleri inspected her handiwork critically. A little over-baked around the edges, but otherwise as good as Ffion's bakes. Nah, they were perfect. She allowed herself a small, proud smile.

Holding up a finished Welsh cake, Eleri could practically see Ffion grinning and cheering, "Those look perfect, cariad!" She hugged the memory close.

Cleaning the kitchen, Eleri's felt happier than she had in a long time. She had baked dozens of cakes as if blindfolded, following well-worn steps. But this simple act had brought her aunt back to life, if only for a moment.

She stared at the Welsh cakes. They had turned out well - sweet and warm, filled with raisins. It would be a pity to just throw them in the bin. On a whim, she packaged up a few of the still-warm cakes and headed down the winding lane.

She spotted a homeless woman she often passed earlier sitting on the pavement near the shops on the high street. Approaching with a friendly smile, Eleri held out the paper bag. "Fresh baked this minute if you'd like some."

The woman's creased face brightened as she took it with gnarled hands. "Bless you, cariad."

Suddenly her eyes darkened, grip clenching Eleri's arm painfully tight. Eleri gasped. The woman's voice dropped to an ominous rasp: "You've been given a gift, girl, even if it's hard to understand right now."

Just as quickly, her expression cleared, her hold relaxing. Eleri staggered back, pulse racing. She stared at the woman, but she had already begun munching a cake, oblivious.

Shaken, Eleri backed away. She rubbed her throbbing arm, unable to shake the woman's strange warning. What had she meant about a gift? But the woman simply smiled and waved goodbye, the cryptic moment gone.

Eleri rubbed her arm and turned to leave. She caught sight of Gareth crouched nearby, speaking with a homeless man. Their eyes met and Gareth stood, surprise flashing across his face.

"I didn't know you helped the homeless on top of running your shop," Eleri said, touched that Gareth volunteered his time this way.

He shrugged, glancing away, almost shy. "I try to do what I can. My mam always said our purpose is to leave the world a little better."

Gareth had a good heart under that rugged exterior. She was seeing him in a new light since returning home. Clearing her throat, Eleri said goodbye and continued down the lane, sneaking a glance back to see Gareth watching her walk away.

The next morning, Eleri slid the last tray of scones into the display case with satisfaction. She had descended the stairs before dawn to prepare the morning pastries. Now delicious aromas filled the shop, ready to welcome customers.

As Eleri arranged artful towers of scones in the front window, she froze. Gareth strolled by outside, hands in his pockets. Her pulse quickened.

The door jangled as Mary breezed in. "Morning, Eleri!" she sang out. Her bright smile faded when she saw Eleri's expression. "You alright?"

Eleri blinked and turned away from the window. "Yes, sorry.

Just thought I saw someone."

Mary followed her gaze but seemed to think better of prying. "Well, I'm famished! What do you recommend?"

Eleri's tension eased as she helped her friend choose a selection of cakes. They settled at the window table.

Mary bit into a scone and sighed contentedly. "Mmm, to die for. They rival your aunt's."

"Thanks." Eleri smiled, sipping her tea. "I've been rehearsing them nonstop. Feels good to see people enjoying the fruits of my labour."

"Well, keep it up because these are brilliant." Mary licked crumbs from her fingers. "Have you put any thought yet into decor and furnishings and all that?"

Eleri grimaced. "I've been so focused on the baking and the cleaning. To be honest, I know the dining area needs some sprucing up, but I'm almost broke. I can't afford to go to the shops."

She glanced around at the simple wooden chairs and tables. The mint walls were cheery but bare. Vintage charm met minimalist style.

"It's looking rather plain, isn't it?" Mary said. "Lacking some, well... personality."

Eleri nodded, feeling glum.

"You know, you should ask Gareth for help," Mary suggested. "His antique shop is brimming with wonderful items. I bet he'd offer you great deals."

Eleri bit her lip, considering. They had such history, both sweet and complicated. Was she ready to deepen their renewed connection?

"It's just a thought." Mary took a swig of tea, looking over the mug's brim. "His style would suit this place, and not all his stuff is actual expensive antiques."

Mary had a point. Blending new beginnings and nostalgia felt fitting for the bakery. And who better than Gareth to understand that?

"I'll reach out to him," Eleri decided. Mary smiled encouragingly.

Chapter 3

The door jangled, and Gareth glanced up from the vase he was examining. He nearly dropped it when he saw Eleri walk in. Eleri. Here. He still couldn't believe she was here after all these years.

Don't gawk, he scolded himself, setting the vase down with care and striding over. A professional welcome is needed here, he thought. He displayed no hint of the avalanche of emotions now coursing through him.

"Eleri, what a pleasant surprise," he managed in a calm tone, gesturing for her to step into the back office. Safe neutral ground, for whatever business matter had brought her unannounced back into his world after a decade.

"Fancy a cuppa?" He asked.

"Lovely," she replied.

"Be right back." Gareth ducked into the small kitchen, where steam still whispered from the kettle. He plucked two tea bags from the caddy and nestled them in the waiting antique teapot. The fragrance of black tea soon infused the air as the bags steeped.

Gareth carefully assembled the tray - floral teacups clinking alongside a small milk jug and sugar bowl. He focused on keeping his hands steady, hyperaware of Eleri waiting in the next room.

Tray loaded, he navigated down the narrow hallway, concentrating to avoid spilling. When he entered the office, Eleri still occupied the chair, lost in thought. At the click of china, she glanced up as he offered a tentative smile. Perhaps over tea, they could continue chipping away at the wall between them.

The worn leather wing-backed chairs creaked beneath them

as Eleri and Gareth settled in. He focused on keeping his gaze natural, as he poured the hot tea into the cups, despite the way his pulse quickened whenever their eyes met. There was something about Eleri that had captivated him. Ever since they were kids. It was a spark, a love of life, and possibly that gorgeous red hair. He averted his eyes, picking up his tea to distract his hands.

"I want to preserve the cafe like Aunt Ffion wanted it, while also putting my own stamp on the bakery," Eleri explained. Her pale hands moved through the air gracefully, catching the afternoon sunlight streaming through the back windows. She sounded like she was trying to convince a banker to give her a loan.

Gareth nodded, clasping his hands tightly together in his lap to resist reaching out and catching her restless fingers in his own.

"Maybe I'll rename some of her classics, like Ffion's Famous Scones could become Eleri's Delightful Scones, or make my own Eleri's Wonderful Welsh Cakes."

The corners of Gareth's mouth twitched at the names.

"I'd be delighted to help," he said. They spent the next hour wandering the shelves, with Eleri pulling out potential pieces, as he described each item's history. Don't stare at the way the light catches her hair, he reminded himself. This was about the antiques.

After Eleri left, Gareth strode through the shop alone, trailing his fingers over the surfaces Eleri had touched. He could help her, he realised. There was plenty here that he could offer at cost that would suit her little bakery cafe.

The next week, he texted Eleri photos of recent additions he thought she might like - a stand of iron hooks curved like vines, floral oil paintings gilt-framed. The enthused responses reassured him, making him want to help her all the more.

A few days later, Gareth entered the bakery to find Eleri already bustling about. Her cheerful "Good morning!" made his heart skip despite himself. Get it together, Gareth chided himself, taking a bracing breath. They had work to do. Side by side, they tackled, transforming the dingy space into Eleri's vision; hanging framed paintings, draping colourful cloths, putting up hooks. Gareth explained each antique's history as they worked. He wanted to help shape an environment as welcoming as Eleri herself. Watching her flit around, he felt invested in making this venture succeed for her sake.

When Eleri hugged him later, the touch nearly undid all his restraint. Careful, he warned himself, as their eyes locked. Not yet. She might not feel the same way. She'd chosen John, not him. Patience, he reminded himself. If it was meant to be, the perfect moment would come.

Chapter 4

The next morning, Eleri busied herself preparing the bakery kitchen. She gathered ingredients and tied on an apron, eager to dive into Ffion's recipes.

As she organised her tools, Eleri's gaze fell on the giant commercial stand mixer dominating the centre counter. Ffion had called "Ol' Bessie" for its workhorse reliability over decades.

It was still working perfectly, but she needed something smaller as well. She wanted to cook cakes for people with allergies, and cleaning that hulking appliance felt too much like hard work. Ol' Bessie wasn't ideal for small batches - or thorough cleans after every batch!

Eleri chewed her lip thoughtfully. A smaller mixer would be better. Second-hand shops sometimes had options. And she couldn't afford to buy new. Her thoughts immediately went to Gareth. A small voice in the back of her mind whispered that she was only inventing an excuse to visit Gareth again. Eleri pushed the notion away. No, she needed to see him. If she was going to make this thing a success, she had to cater for everyone.

Cleaning her hands on her apron, she hung it up on a peg on her way out, grabbing her coat at the same time. Eleri hurried down the alley to his antique shop. The door jangled as she entered.

Gareth looked up from polishing a table and broke into a grin. "Eleri! Twice in one week - to what do I owe the pleasure?"

"Bore da, Gareth." Eleri smiled, happy to see him so soon again too. "I've got another favour to ask."

"Name it." Gareth set down his cloth and leaned against the

table, his lean, muscular frame on unconscious display.

"Well, I was cooking this morning and realised my kitchen could use some smaller equipment as well, something that I can keep separate," Eleri explained. She tried not to notice how Gareth's shirt hugged his chest. "Especially a stand mixer - Ol' Bessie is great, but she's ancient. I need something which I can put on the other counter, so I don't contaminate food and accidentally kill someone. Know of any anything that could work? I know I'm asking a lot."

Gareth rubbed his stubbled chin thoughtfully. "I don't have any in stock currently. But I'll put my feelers out, see what surfaces."

Eleri breathed out a long, low breath. "That's amazing, thank you. I'd like something with charm but also functional."

"You got it. Something small, that looks good, and works." Gareth counted the items off his fingers and then shot her a playful salute. "Aye aye, captain. I will scour the seven seas for the perfect match, or at least Ceredigion."

He mimed swashbuckling with an invisible sword, making her laugh. "I solemnly swear as a knight of the antique roundtable to track down a quality second hand mixer for the fair maiden Eleri."

"You might have mixed up your metaphors there, mate."

"I see what you did there," he replied with a wink.

With a parting wave, Eleri headed back down the lane, smiling to herself. She loved these moments with Gareth.

Over the next week, the search for kitchen items continued. Gareth messaged Eleri constantly with questions to make sure what he was finding out would be right for her.

She smiled down at her phone during a slow moment one afternoon. His latest text showed a photo of an aqua mixer circa 1960.

Eleri quickly typed back, detailing the size and attachments she needed. She relied on Gareth. He seemed to know what she needed.

Soon he responded with a thumbs up emoji and promised to

keep looking. Eleri clutched her phone, a smile growing.

A few days later, Eleri was whisking batter when she heard the shop door open.

"Eleri?" Gareth's voice called out. "You back there?"

"In the kitchen!" She set down the bowl to peek out and saw him wheeling in a large object draped in a sheet.

"Got a little delivery for you," he said with a playful grin.

Eleri pulled off the sheet, then gasped. Before her stood a gleaming stand mixer in cheery sunshine yellow.

"Gareth, it's absolutely gorgeous!" She turned the smooth chrome knobs and tested the sturdy lever.

"Mid-century. Just tuned up and running like a dream," he said, pleased by her reaction. "The yellow reminded me of your smile."

Eleri glanced up, cheeks warming. "You put so much thought into finding me just the right thing. I can't thank you enough."

Gareth waved dismissively. "It's nothing. I enjoy the hunt." He held her gaze. "And I want to help however I can."

Eleri's heart leapt. She had an impulse to embrace him again but settled for resting a hand on his arm briefly. "You've been wonderful. Please send me your invoice for this."

"On the house." Gareth backed away, hands raised before she could protest. "Friends and family discount. I insist."

"Feels more like I'm getting a five fingered discount," she joked.

He laughed and sauntered out with a parting wink. Eleri leaned against the counter, pulse skittering. She knew Gareth was just being kind. But sometimes it felt like more.

Over the next week, Eleri put the mixer to good use, experimenting with new recipes, batches of biscuits, banana muffins, and other cakes for the grand reopening. She found herself continually distracted by thoughts of when she might see Gareth again. She could feel whispers trying to break into her awareness, but working helped to block them out.

One morning, Eleri was decorating cupcakes. She heard a familiar voice in the café, greeting Mary. She dropped the icing bag, using her apron to clean her hands as she pushed through the swing door.

"Bore da, ladies!" Gareth strode forward, wheeling a large object covered by a sheet. He stopped by her friend sitting on a bar stool at the counter. "Got another delivery for you, Eleri."

"Ooh, unveil the mystery!" Mary said, eyes twinkling with curiosity, her fingers reaching out to pull the sheet. Gareth playfully slapped her hand away. She grinned, unrepentant.

With a flourish, Gareth whipped off the sheet to reveal a gleaming professional oven. Eleri gasped, hands covering her mouth.

"Stunning, isn't it?" Gareth ran a hand along the cool steel exterior. "It's only a year old. I got it from a bakery that closed in Llangurig. They delivered it this morning."

"It's... incredible," Eleri managed, overwhelmed. She stepped around the counter, circled the oven, admiring the polished chrome details. "That's second hand?"

He rubbed the back of his neck, glancing away. "Well, your kitchen is shaping up nicely. Just a few more finishing touches needed."

Their eyes met, and Eleri hoped her gratitude shone through. "Please send me your invoice. I insist on paying for this. It's too much."

Gareth opened his mouth to protest, but Eleri silenced him with a raised finger. "I won't take no for an answer. I know you gave me a friend discount before. But I'm running a business now, so let me do this properly."

With a small smile, Gareth nodded. "You drive a hard bargain. Invoice coming your way." He tipped an imaginary hat at her and Mary before departing.

Eleri's insides fizzed like shaken champagne. She wanted to run after Gareth and throw her arms around him. But she contented herself with giggling with Mary.

Over the next few days, Eleri felt upbeat and energised. The new equipment opened possibilities for recipes and events. She brainstormed menu items and decor touches.

When Gareth's invoice arrived, Eleri gladly paid it, adding

a little something extra as another gesture of thanks. There had to be something more she could do to show how grateful she was for everything he had done. But what? She wanted it to be meaningful, from the heart. With Gareth, she never had to search for words. Expressing herself came naturally, just as their connection had fallen back into place so seamlessly after all this time.

Wiping her hands, Eleri headed down the winding lane to Aber Antiques. The door chimed cheerfully as she entered the charming shop.

Gareth leaned against the front counter, brows furrowed as he studied a ledger. He glanced up, face breaking into a grin.

"Eleri, prynhawn da! What brings you here today then?" He set aside the book with a welcoming gesture.

"Hello, Gareth. I'm hunting for some decorations to finish off the cafe, now I've got all the practical stuff. Thought I'd browse your wares for inspiration. I've also brought you this cake as a thank you for all you've done."

She brought out the box she'd been hiding behind her back.

"That's lovely! Diolch. Wonderful idea, cariad." Gareth took the box and eagerly motioned her further inside. "Let's explore the treasures."

They meandered through the cluttered aisles and alcoves. Eleri admired items along the way - ornate mirrors, paintings of seascapes, a display of crystal accessories.

"Ooh, look at these!" She lifted a set of delicate porcelain teacups decorated with trailing vines.

"Lovely, aren't they?" Gareth smiled indulgently as she turned each cup to inspect the details. "Early 1900s, I believe."

Eleri pictured dainty ladies in gowns sipping from these, over polite conversation. The floral patterns and graceful shapes encapsulated the essence of a bygone era.

"I think these would be perfect on the bakery shelves." Eleri returned the teacups to their velvet-lined box.

Gareth's expression turned hesitant. "Are you sure? Those are quite valuable. I'd worry about potential damage with daily use in a busy cafe."

Eleri considered, then nodded. "You make a good point. I'd hate for anything to happen to them. Maybe I'll go with something sturdier."

"Wise choice." Gareth's warm approval sent a tingle down her spine. "Let's keep exploring then."

They continued browsing through the maze of items. Turning a corner revealed a shelf of old cookbooks.

Eleri clasped her hands in delight. "These are fabulous! Ffion would have loved them."

She trailed her fingers along the spines, sounding out the titles.

"Cookbooks are perfect since they won't get damaged by customers." Gareth hovered nearby, observing her reactions with a tender expression. "And I bet you'll find some recipe inspiration."

"I already have, thank you!" Eleri flipped through the pages, admiring handwritten notes crammed in margins.

Gareth insisted on giving her a steep discount, waving off her attempts to pay full price. As Eleri loaded her purchases, she bubbled over with descriptive plans for displaying the books open to feature recipes.

One crisp afternoon, Eleri was arranging a display of cake stands when the shop bell announced Gareth's arrival.

"Don't look yet!" she called out. With a last change, she stepped back and surveyed her work. "Okay, you can come see."

Gareth let out an impressed whistle as he rounded the corner. "This looks amazing, cariad."

His gaze travelled over the cookbooks propped open to recipes, framed photos, and china displays. "It has so much character. Just like your aunt would've done."

Eleri's eyes misted over. "Do you think so? That was my hope."

"Absolutely." Gareth moved closer and spoke in a gentle voice. "Her spirit is alive here because of you."

Overwhelmed by emotion, Eleri embraced him. Gareth's arms wrapped around her soothingly as she whispered,

"Thank you."

Stepping back, Eleri dabbed her eyes and laughed. "Sorry about that."

"Don't be." Gareth's brown eyes were tender. "I know how much she meant to you. I'm honoured I could help bring part of her back."

After a lingering moment of connection, Gareth insisted on taking Eleri to the pub for a celebratory pint. Settled into a cosy booth, they talked for hours about childhood escapades, lost dreams and bright beginnings.

Eleri marvelled at how easily she opened up to Gareth. The intervening years since their teens seemed to disappear. It felt meant to be, their paths crossing again when she needed his friendship the most.

As they strolled back, Eleri impulsively slipped her hand into Gareth's. He gave a small surprised smile, then interlaced their fingers.

Eleri's heart overflowed with contentment. With Gareth, the future somehow felt bright and hopeful, no matter the obstacles ahead. She'd made the right decision to come back.

"Oh Eleri, it looks wonderful!" Mary enthused as she breezed in the next morning. "So, chic!"

Eleri grinned. "Gareth provided most of it. Wasn't that lovely of him?"

Mary gave her a knowing look. "What a thoughtful gesture. That man certainly seems very interested in helping you succeed."

Ignoring her friend's implication, Eleri busied herself brewing tea. She wasn't ready to examine what might lie behind Gareth's ongoing generosity. He wasn't interested in her like that. He was just a friend.

She smiled and closed the door behind Mary as she left with a knowing look. Suddenly the lights flickered, and the radio crackled to life, making Eleri jump. Heart pounding, she glanced around the empty bakery. As her eyes adjusted to the dim lighting, she spotted a shadowy figure standing behind the counter.

An eerie whispering filled the air, growing louder. Eleri clutched her hands over her ears, eyes squeezed shut. "Not again. Stop it, please!" she cried out, tears slipping down her cheeks. The ominous whispers continued their haunting chorus as Eleri sank down against the door into a shaking ball.

After what felt like an eternity, the murmurs faded away. Eleri hesitantly looked up to find the bakery bathed in light again, looking perfectly normal. She took a shaky breath, wiping the dampness from her cheeks with trembling fingers. The shadowy figure and creepy whispers had vanished like ghosts.

***

Eleri was pricing baked goods when the shop bell tinkled. They looked up to see Gareth wheeling in a vintage glass-fronted bakery cabinet.

"Gareth! You shouldn't have," Eleri exclaimed, rushing over.

"What do you think?" He gestured to the cabinet proudly. "I refinished this piece myself. It can display drinks and cookbooks perfectly in that spare spot in the cafe area."

Gareth waved off her effusive thanks as he helped position the cabinet. Eleri tried offering payment again, but he refused. "I want to contribute however I can. This old thing needs more love."

His sincerity stirred feelings Eleri wasn't prepared to confront. To distract herself, she opened the cookbooks he'd displayed inside the cabinet.

"These are perfect!" She turned the fragile pages reverently.

Gareth smiled. "I hoped you'd like them."

Mary looked at her friend helplessly as Gareth walked out.

"Oh, come on! He's obviously into you. How many times has he come in here? There's personal service, and then there's what Gareth is doing. You know he doesn't do house calls, don't you? He's not a doctor!"

"He's just being friendly, Mary." Eleri dismissed her friend's comments. Mary rolled her eyes and grabbed her bag on her way out. A chill filled the air and Eleri shivered as she felt a pressure grow at the fringes of her mind. This. Would. Not. Happen. She clenched her hands, and the whispers receded.

Over the next week, Eleri and Gareth fell into easy collaboration, as he continued supplying accent pieces. His enthusiasm was contagious as he explained the history behind each item while helping her artfully arrange them. In return, she 'donated' a few of Aunt Ffion's things that she wouldn't miss.

Watching his strong hands polish the wooden counter or hang frames with care revealed hidden layers to this man, who had always been in the background. It stirred a tender feeling in Eleri she hadn't expected.

One Sunday morning when Eleri arrived to decorate, she discovered an antique cash register outside the front door with a note:

Eleri - found this classic piece and thought it would be perfect here. Let me know if you need any help to set it up. Yours, Gareth.

She caressed the ornate brass buttons and intricate embossing. The warmth of his ongoing thoughtfulness enveloped her like a cosy blanket.

When Gareth dropped by later, Eleri rushed to hug him. "I don't know how to thank you for your generosity," she said into his shoulder.

Gareth rubbed her back. "Your happiness is thanks enough." He pulled back to gaze at her solemnly. "I meant it when I said I'd help any way I can. Whenever and however you need me."

Eleri's breath caught at the intensity in his brown eyes. Before she could respond, he squeezed her shoulders and stepped away to examine the register setup.

As Eleri watched him work, her earlier resolution to do something special for Gareth resurfaced. His continual help had been invaluable. She wanted to express what it meant to her in a meaningful, personal way. Her aunt would have insisted on reciprocating such kindness.

Eleri sank onto the velvet settee in the flat, exhausted. Lately the ghosts followed her everywhere, their eerie whispers invading her mind the second she was alone. She massaged her throbbing temples, fighting off another tension headache.

It was only when she was with Gareth or Mary that she found respite from the haunting. Their lively company kept the spirits at bay. But their presence could only distract her for so long.

Being with Gareth or Mary helped distract her from the relentless haunting. But their lively company only kept the spirits at bay temporarily.

As Eleri stared aimlessly at the empty fireplace, her gaze snagged on Aunt Ffion's urn. She jolted upright, pulse kicking. The urn! How had she not thought of it sooner?

Eleri jumped up, galvanised by sudden purpose. She knew exactly what needed to be done to banish the ghosts for good. The solution was right in front of her this whole time.

Chapter 5

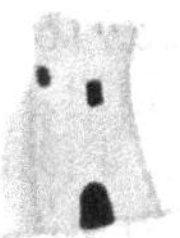

The morning sun peeked through the curtains, casting slices of light across Eleri's face. She opened her eyes, momentarily forgetting the weight that had settled on her shoulders until the previous night came flooding back.

Today was the day she would follow Aunt Ffion's final wish.

Eleri dressed methodically, focusing on each button to keep her nerves at bay. She brewed a strong cup of tea, hoping the bracing liquid would steady her hands. The ceramic urn, painted with seashells, seemed to sit almost expectantly on the kitchen table, with an air of reproof.

"Just a little longer, Aunt," Eleri whispered, caressing the vessel that held her aunt's ashes. She could almost hear Ffion's gentle laughter on the breeze drifting through the open window.

The bakery's faded floral wallpaper blurred as Eleri's mind drifted back to that cramped solicitor's office. She could still smell the cloying cigar smoke absorbed into the leather furniture, hear the clock ticking with an ominous hollow sound on the wall. Her hands gripped together in her lap as the stern solicitor droned on, reading Ffion's will in a monotonous voice. Most of the words blurred together meaninglessly until:

"I wish for my ashes to be spread into the sea, returning me to the waters I so love."

She saw why she'd chosen the urn design now. A hint of her wishes. She picked up the simple ceramic urn, hefting its weight, imagining the ashes longing for their resting place among the waves. The memory pierced her heart, those words echoing painfully in her mind. She blinked rapidly, the floral wallpaper coming back into focus.

Eleri could almost see her aunt uttering those words, her

eyes shining like the ever-changing sea whenever she gazed at the waves. Her reddish-brown hair almost glowing in the sun. The sea was where Ffion had felt most alive, most free. It called to her spirit like a siren song.

And now Eleri understood the duty her aunt had entrusted her with. She must reunite Ffion's spirit with those eternal waters. If she admitted the truth, it should have been the first thing she did when she got back. But she hadn't been ready to say goodbye.

The walk wasn't far. She decided that the sandy area by the pier was the best place. It was never very busy there, and it was where they had escaped to so often, just the two of them.

Eleri cradled the urn as she plodded down the pavement, each step heavy yet purposeful. She absently noted the clouds gathering above her. Rain would come soon - as if the sky was sympathetic to her mood.

The familiar crunch of shells and stones beneath her worn shoes soothed Eleri's fraying nerves. She inhaled, filling her lungs with the bracing coastal air. The briny scent conjured carefree childhood days spent beach combing with Gareth, hunting for seashells. She could almost hear his boyish laughter above the crashing waves.

How long ago that seemed, before life's changes and tragedies had swept in like the remorseless tide. Eleri sighed, her breath lost to the quickening wind. She'd lost so much time, years chasing a dream in London she didn't even want. This is where she wanted, needed to be.

She reached the deserted beach, a peaceful crescent of sand tucked between weathered cliffs. Her and Ffion's refuge, their happy place. Eleri knelt on the sand, letting the coarse grains sift through her fingers - just as she and Gareth had done while building elaborate sandcastles here so long ago. She absently sketched wavy lines in the sand, her heart aching at the memories.

Raindrops began to dimple the beach around her, lending quiet urgency to Eleri's task. She looked out at the dark swells roiling beneath the granite sky. The first glimpse of a rising dawn in the distance. It was time. It felt right.

With trembling fingers, Eleri unsealed the urn. The ashes appeared almost reluctant to leave their shelter, swirling lazily inside.

"It's time, Aunt," Eleri whispered. She blinked against the sting of tears.

Scooping up a handful of fine grey ash, Eleri cast it into the waiting waves. The silvery fragments hung suspended, as if hesitating. Then a sudden gust swept them back onto the shore, the ashes swirling around Eleri in a delicate shroud. She staggered back in horror as her aunt's remains billowed towards her, coating her skin and clothes in a chilling caress.

She froze, arms still outstretched. The wind swirled around her, whisking the ashes into eddies. Eyes closed, Eleri could almost imagine she had become the ghostly village spirit Aunt Ffion delighted in telling stories about over steaming mugs of hot chocolate.

As Eleri's brain cottoned on to what happened, she staggered back, horrified. The ashes coated her everywhere. Eleri spat frantically as the ash invaded her mouth. Flailing her hands to brush it off.

Then she paused, a smile crept onto her face as realisation dawned - this must be Aunt Ffion's doing. One last mischievous laugh from beyond.

"Couldn't resist just one more cwtch goodbye, eh Aunt?" Eleri laughed, now gently brushing the ashes away with care, reverence replacing repulsion.

She could practically see her aunt's wrinkled nose crinkling with mirth at this parting gesture. "I forgive you that one, cariad," Eleri chuckled. She blew a kiss out to the waves. Her aunt always had a wicked sense of humour.

As the last ashen traces fell away, Eleri noticed the rain had turned into a faint drizzle. The clouds were already thinning, revealing glimpses of blue sky between their fraying edges.

Eleri tore her gaze from the churning sea. A sudden slash of sunlight through the clouds drew her attention down the beach. She squinted and made out a glint half-buried in the sand.

Eleri set the urn aside and gently swept the grains away. There was something there. A tarnished silver locket emerged, dangling from a fragile, weathered chain. Eleri lifted it carefully, brushing off flecks of grit until the pendant shone despite its age.

Eleri's breath became trapped in her throat. She recognised this - it had belonged to Aunt Ffion. As a child, Eleri had marvelled over the intricate knotwork engraving on the tarnished surface. Ffion had always worn it close to her heart. Until one day it was lost to the sea.

Reverently, Eleri cradled the damaged locket in her palm. The cold metal seemed to hum against her skin, as if whispering all the secrets it had witnessed over the decades.

She ran her fingers over the Celtic knot patterns, picturing her aunt's weathered hands doing the same so many times. A lump formed in Eleri's throat. This small talisman encompassed so much lost history.

Driven by some incomprehensible instinct, Eleri fumbled to open the fragile clasp. The locket fell open with a click, the years of grit finally giving way. Inside was not a photo, as she had imagined, but a tiny, exquisitely detailed painting of a striking young woman with the red hair of her family and laughing eyes. Eleri's breath caught - the woman looked exactly like a younger version of her Aunt Ffion.

Eleri stared, transfixed by this ghost from the past. As she did, the edges of her vision started to blur and shift, like the tide pools receding into the sand. The empty beach morphed into a bustling scene from another era. Elegantly dressed people, in regency style, strolled arm in arm down the boardwalk and piers. Among them was the red-haired woman from the painting, her eyes full of life as she gazed out to sea.

Eleri clutched the locket tighter, willing the vision to continue, hungry to understand this glimpse into the past. But as quickly as it came, the shimmering scene dissolved away. Eleri was left standing alone again on the windy beach, with more questions than answers.

She placed the locket in her pocket, the hard metal a reminder of her aunt. Determined to cherish the memory, she vowed to have it restored and wear it daily.

Eleri returned to the urn resting in the sand. This time, when she took a handful of ashes, the wind did not intervene. The fine particles floated across the water, disappearing into the low waves with tender reverence.

As Eleri tipped the last vestiges into the tide, she whispered, "Be free, Aunt. Diolch for everything."

The empty urn felt light in Eleri's hands as she watched the final swirling eddies dissipate into the murky bay. It was done. Ffion was home again, her spirit one with her beloved ocean. The clouds had broken fully, bathing the cove in ephemeral morning sunlight.

Eleri knew her aunt would not have wanted tears or a lingering goodbye. So, she simply knelt and touched her fingers to the water lapping the shore, sending one last wish into the salty foam.

"Happy travels, Ffion. I love you."

As the sunlight broke through the gloom, washing the world in renewed colour and hope, cars appeared on the road and people walked their dogs. She climbed back up the incline, marvelling at how much lighter she felt. Her aunt's spirit would always be with her, present in each wave and every grain of sand.

Chapter 6

Gareth glared at the empty ledger, anxiety mounting as another day ticked by without a single customer. Helping Eleri with the bakery had become his sole bright spot lately. Though her own sales were slow, she still paid generously for his antique supplies, even though she had no idea about his financial situation. Her cheerful presence was a welcome distraction from his dire financial situation.

But it pained Gareth to watch Eleri work so hard to buoy them both. He longed to ask her on a real date - a nice meal together would lift their spirits. And maybe spark fresh ideas to revive the shop. Still, he hesitated, not wanting to be a further burden. For now, her friendship alone was a gift.

Gareth sighed, glancing outside at the vacant street. He had to turn things around, if not for himself, then for Eleri. She believed in him, and he couldn't let her down. The answer was out there somewhere. He just had to dig deep and find it.

A knock at the door jarred him from his brooding. To his surprise, Eleri stood on the step, holding a weathered wooden box. Wordlessly, she led him inside and opened the box. Nestled inside was a delicate silver locket on a braided chain. He instantly recognised it.

Gareth's breath caught. "That locket... do you know its legend?"

Curiosity flickered in her eyes. "Legend? What legend?"

He leaned closer, his voice almost a whisper. "They say that locket was once worn by star-crossed lovers. The key to unlocking a hidden treasure. Some believe it holds the power to reunite souls destined to be together."

Eleri's heart skipped a beat, and an image of the young woman who looked like Aunt Ffion wearing the locket on the pier flashed through her mind. What was the connection? She wondered if this locket could be the same.

Reverently, Gareth lifted the locket from the box. His thumb traced the intricate knotwork engraved on the surface. Hands trembling, he unclasped it and eased the cover open.

Inside was a worn painting of a lady who bore a striking resemblance to Eleri. Gareth's pulse hammered. This was indisputable evidence that Eleri's ancestor was linked to the curse in the book.

"I can't believe it," Eleri whispered. "It just appeared so suddenly..."

Gareth gingerly set the locket down on the table. He abruptly turned and disappeared out the back. Moving several boxes aside, he pulled out an ancient, dusty tome from the bottom one. Returning to Eleri, he placed the book before her and thumbed through the worn pages, stopping at one he had peered at countless times before. The faded parchment crackled as he flattened it out across the weathered wooden counter, twisting it with a flourish to face her. Anticipation glinted in his eyes. He tapped the page.

Beside the book, the locket glinted in the afternoon sun streaming through the shop window, its silver surface engraved with intricate Celtic knotwork. Gareth's eyes darted between the pendant resting on the counter and the drawing in the aged book laid open beside it. He looked at Eleri, willing her to see it. The images matched perfectly. This was unmistakably the enchanted locket described in the old Welsh legends.

"We need to examine every detail," he murmured. "There must be clues about how to unlock its power."

Eleri's brows furrowed, confusion plain on her face. "Its power? What are you on about?"

Gareth hesitated, unsure how much to reveal. But the hope kindling in his chest won out.

"That locket is famous around here. I've been searching for it for years. Never thought it would just be... found." He met her gaze questioning.

Eleri nodded. "I found it in the sand this morning. I brought it straight here, figured you were the one to ask about it. But what's all this about a power?"

Gareth leaned in; voice hushed. "Legend says that locket holds the key to breaking a centuries-old curse. If the right person finds it before Christmas Eve, they can break a curse."

"You can't be serious," Eleri gasped. But goosebumps prickled her arms, memories of the strange dreams and visions surfacing unbidden. The young woman on the pier, wearing that very locket... The whispers, maybe she was cursed?

Gareth took the pendant in hand, fingertips tracing the intricate engraving. "I've studied the legends for years. Finding this now must be fate."

"She looks just like you," he breathed. "It's your ancestor, linked to the curse."

Eleri stared wide-eyed at the tiny portrait. "That's not me. It looks like Ffion. And curse? What curse?"

Gareth hesitated only a moment before grabbing another leather-bound book from under the counter. He flipped through the pages covered in spidery handwritten Welsh, translating passages as he scanned.

"A powerful curse kept your ancestor, Angharad, and her fiancée Rhys apart. His life was cut short. She blamed the curse, but it says here that the locket holds the key to reuniting their souls and breaking the curse's hold for good."

He looked up, eyes ablaze. "This curse is centuries old. It can only be stopped if the right descendant finds it before Christmas Eve. That's you, Eleri."

Her head spun, struggling to reconcile these revelations with logic. Curses and enchanted lockets belonged in fantasy, not the real world. But real or not, Gareth looked like he believed the legend. And she couldn't deny the uncanny resemblances and visions urging her on.

Swallowing hard, she met his fervent gaze. "If this curse is real... how do we break it?"

Gareth's face broke into a grin. "The clues must be hidden in the locket's design. Help me decipher them?"

Eleri nodded, heart hammering as he spread the two books

open. What answers were in their crumbling pages? Could it hold the power to get rid of the voices?

For hours they pored over the texts, examining each intricate knot and symbol, Gareth's excitement growing with every possible link uncovered. Eleri blinked gritty eyes as the light faded, head aching from concentration.

"We should pick this up tomorrow," she said finally, stifling a yawn. "It's getting late."

Gareth frowned, reluctant to stop. But he closed the books with a sigh.

"First thing tomorrow, then. We're so close, I can feel it." He clasped her hand tightly. "This will work, Eleri. We'll solve it together."

She offered a tired smile in return, wishing she shared his conviction. Troubling doubts lurked beneath her curiosity. What if this magic was beyond their control?

They parted ways outside the shop, the inky night sky dusted with stars. Eleri shivered as she walked, unsure if it was from the evening chill or apprehension coiling in her gut. She glanced over her shoulder, unable to shake the sense of unseen eyes tracking her path through the empty streets.

When she arrived home, the locket felt heavy in her coat pocket. Lying in bed, Eleri studied the portrait of her so-called ancestor, so it wasn't Ffion, but one of their ancestors. She felt more unsettled than ever. What did she have to do with the legend? And how much should she trust Gareth's feverish belief in curses and enchantments?

Restless, she rose and crossed to the flat window overlooking the moonlit bay. The dark waters glinted like liquid silver. Somewhere beneath their inky depths lay the answers she sought.

As her eyes scanned the shadows along the shoreline, a pale figure stepped into the moonlight. Heart seizing, Eleri recognised the young woman from her visions, auburn hair whipping in the wind. The locket glinted at her throat as she gazed up at Eleri. Then her lips moved in a silent message.

"Break the curse."

She gestured urgently towards the sea, then turned and vanished into the darkness once more. Eleri stumbled back, pulse racing. Was she going mad, or had she seen her ancestor's spirit?

Why couldn't Ffion just tell them what to do? Frustration built within her, making her ball her fists in anger. What was the point of seeing ghosts if they were just going to be cryptic? If Gareth was right, the deadline loomed - she had to break this mysterious curse by Christmas Eve. But how? The spirits had given no explicit instructions, only vague warnings. She racked her brain trying to piece it together, but time was running out. If she failed, then she would never be free of the voices and her family would be cursed forever.

Chapter 7

Eleri hummed tunelessly to herself, focused on measuring ingredients for her new scone recipe. The rich scents of cinnamon filled the warm bakery kitchen. She had gone downstairs early, eager to test new flavour ideas that had come to her in an inspired rush last night. Her regulars would be eager to try the free samples.

Kneading the dough, she pictured her customers' delighted faces biting into the scones. She loved her job. She didn't love that she waited until she was 28 to do her dream, but life was what it was. This little bakery she had inherited from Aunt Ffion was her home now. She would not worry about a curse that she couldn't do anything about. The bakery was doing well. Gareth and Mary were amazing friends, and she could block out the voices if she tried.

The front bell chimed, interrupting Eleri's contented reverie. She dusted off her floury hands and headed to the front, expecting one of her regulars. But she froze mid-step when she saw John standing just inside the entrance.

Her breath caught in her throat as a wave of emotions crashed over her - confusion, apprehension, and a flare of that old hurt she thought had faded. What was he doing here after all these months of silence? She watched warily as he took a hesitant step forward, his eyes clouded with what looked like regret. Or was it just nostalgia for what he had carelessly tossed aside?

"Eleri..." His voice sent tension coiling up her spine. She noticed the expensive wool of his suit, the flashy watch that had always seemed designed to impress rather than reflect his practical accountant's nature.

"I made a mistake, letting you go." His words dropped into the space between them like stones. Mistake. Letting her go.

As if she were a faulty asset, disposed of and now recalled. She pressed her lips together, smothering the swell of old pain. She would not let him unsettle the new life she had created here.

John ran his fingers through his hair, his shoes shining luxuriously against the scuffed bakery floor. "Losing you made me realise what we had," he declared fervently. What we had. Eleri tensed, bracing herself against the expected onslaught of his soaring romantic overtures that had always masked his lack of substance. Not this time. She wasn't going to fall for it. They'd said everything that needed to be said back in London.

Gareth sat at a small café table at the corner table, sipping his coffee and skimming the news on his phone. He came here most mornings, drawn by the atmosphere and tantalising scents drifting from the kitchen. And if he was honest, by the chance to see Eleri's bright smile when she greeted him.

This morning, he had arrived just as Eleri was heading into the back, flashing him a distracted wave before disappearing through the swinging doors, her red ponytail swinging behind her. He didn't mind. He was happy just being here. Helping himself to the coffeepot behind the counter, he dropped a fiver into the till.

The front door chimed, and Gareth glanced up. His stomach sank when he saw the man standing stiffly just inside the entrance, taking in the quaint cafe with a slight curl to his lip. He was the sort of slick, tailored corporate type that set Gareth's teeth on edge. Who was this guy? A customer? Then he looked closer. It was John! Gareth turned his face away so his old friend wouldn't recognise him.

But John was already turning towards the kitchen door where Eleri was, his face lighting up as she emerged, brushing flour from her hands, only to put white smudges on her face and hair as she brushed strands of her fringe behind her ears.

"Eleri…" John said, voice warm and familiar as he took a step toward her. Gareth tensed, senses on high alert.

Eleri's body language was guarded as she regarded the newcomer. "What are you doing here, John?"

John. The old memories resurfaced. His old rival was back

in town. Gareth sat still, unsure whether to slip out quietly or stay close in case Eleri needed support.

"I made a mistake, letting you go," John was saying now, gazing at Eleri beseechingly. Gareth felt an irrational flare of irritation. It was as if John had magnanimously released her, rather than ignoring her wants and needs.

He shifted in his seat as John took another step closer to Eleri, hand extended. Gareth caught the tight set of her shoulders, the discomfort evident in her face. She needed help to diffuse the situation.

Rising, Gareth cleared his throat. "Everything okay, cariad?" Eleri's eyes flashed to him in surprise, then relief. Moving to her side, Gareth kept his tone mild, hoping she would play along.

"Yes, everything's fine," Eleri replied smoothly, slipping her hand into his. Gareth fought to keep his face neutral at her touch. Inside, his pulse was racing wildly.

"John was just leaving," Eleri said. Gareth forced a polite smile. "Pleased to see you again, John."

John looked between them, stunned. Gareth held his breath, willing the other man to believe their act and retreat. After an endless moment, John's shoulder's slumped in defeat.

"I see. I'm sorry for intruding." Gareth stayed silent as John walked away, risking one last longing look at Eleri before disappearing out the door. Eleri's shoulders slumped in relief.

Gareth released Eleri's hand, missing its warmth immediately. "Thank you," she said gratefully. "I'm sorry to drag you into that."

He chuckled, hoping it sounded natural. "Don't worry about it. That's what friends are for, right?" Friends. Is that all they were? His unruly heart longed for so much more. But now was not the time to confess that.

At Eleri's cheerful offer of coffee and a free scone, Gareth latched on to the opportunity to lighten the mood. Soon they were chatting easily again, the unpleasantness with John fading.

Eleri placed her hand on Gareth's, her touch gentle. "Thank

you for being here since I've returned," she said, her voice above a whisper.

Gareth's pulse quickened at her touch. He willed his voice to remain steady. "Seeing you thrive is thanks enough."

Eleri smiled then, her eyes crinkling with warmth. Gareth's breathing tightened at the sight. He hoped she couldn't see the emotion welling within him, laid bare by that simple gesture. Her hand still rested on his, radiating a comforting heat. He had to fight the urge to grip it, to never let go.

He noticed her gaze flicker briefly, unconsciously, to his mouth, and he gripped his coffee tight to resist the urge to close the distance between them. Patience, he reminded himself, as she hurried back to the safety of the kitchen. There was so much unspoken between them, but the time wasn't right yet. He would know when it was. And then he would finally bare his heart completely.

Over the next few weeks, Gareth found excuses to linger near the bakery, keeping watch for any sign of John darkening the doorstep again. Relief washed over him each day when the man failed to appear.

Gareth couldn't help but smile as he watched Eleri bustle around the bakery, humming cheerfully. Her eyes shone with renewed purpose as she prepared batch after batch of pastries. With each perfect cake and satisfied customer, he could see her confidence growing.

It warmed his heart to witness her passion being reignited. The bakery was clearly more than just a business - it was the realisation of Eleri's lifelong dreams. And knowing he had played some minor role in making that happen filled Gareth with quiet contentment.

Seeing Eleri flourish gave him hope that the antique shop could also have a revival. For now, helping her thrive was satisfaction enough. Her happiness stirred something in him that had been dormant for far too long.

Gareth was careful to keep his own feelings in check. Her well-being was all that mattered for now. He would remain a silent sentinel - ready to intervene again if needed, but content for the moment just to see joy lighting her eyes once more.

But he couldn't deny that his heart leapt each time Eleri flashed him a radiant smile when he entered the bakery. He kept a mental catalogue of the cute way she bit her lip while decorating cakes, the dusting of flour on her nose while baking. Each detail was precious to him.

Still, Gareth hesitated to show how he felt, afraid of disrupting their easy rapport. He contented himself with light conversations as they sipped coffee at the counter while Eleri took her breaks. Making her laugh felt like basking in sunlight.

Yet sometimes he sensed a new softness in Eleri's eyes when she looked at him, noticed her fingers lingering a fraction too long when handing him his coffee. The possibilities tempted him. But patience, he had to remind himself. Let things happen in their own time. John was a complication. What if she still had feelings for him? She'd made it clear, but you couldn't spend ten years with someone without feeling something, surely?

So Gareth tamped down his impatience and continued to be in the present, helping around the bakery wherever he could. Waiting for his moment.

Until then, her friendship was gift enough. Her joy and success here were his, too. Gareth would continue standing as a quiet bulwark against the shadows of Eleri's past, for however long it took for the time to be right. He was in no rush. All that mattered was being ready when she was.

***

Later that afternoon, the summer sun was high after the lunch rush had died down, Eleri flipped the bakery's sign to "Closed" and began tidying up. As she was wiping down tables, Gareth wandered in.

"All right if I come in?" he asked. "Figured you might need some help closing up."

"Please do," said Eleri, gesturing him inside gratefully. She was feeling drained after the morning's events.

They worked in comfortable silence for a few minutes until

the entrance of the bakery was spotless. Eleri brewed them both cups of tea and they settled onto stools at the counter.

Stirring honey into her tea, Eleri shook her head. "I still can't believe John showed up like that. So dramatic."

Gareth nodded sympathetically. "Yeah, seemed like he was laying it on a bit thick. Sure he's not still stuck in his accounting spreadsheets and just sees you as a box to tick off?"

Despite herself, Eleri laughed. "You're probably right. I guess I just wasn't expecting him to come barging back into my life." She hesitated. "And I'm sorry for putting you on the spot, pretending you're my boyfriend."

Gareth busied himself with adding milk to his tea. "Don't worry about it," he said casually. But his eyes were serious. "Unless... you're not actually over, John? I know you used to care about him."

"What? No!" Eleri exclaimed. She leaned towards Gareth earnestly. "That part of my life is over. John was always so wrapped up in his work. He doesn't, he never, even saw me."

Impulsively, she put her hand over Gareth's, where it rested on the counter. His skin was warm and slightly rough under her fingertips.

"You've been the one who's really been there for me since I moved back," Eleri continued. "Not just today with John, but helping me get the bakery running, listening when I was frustrated or unsure of myself..."

She took a long, slow breath. "What I'm trying to say is you're the one I truly care about now, Gareth. Only you."

Gareth turned his hand over to curl his fingers around hers, his eyes intent on her face.

"I care about you too, Eleri," he said. "I know with everything, you've pushed back the grand reopening, but don't you think now would be the time to do it? The tourists are flocking in and we've got nowhere with finding out about the lockets."

"You are right, of course." Her tone was thoughtful. What with John arriving, the curse, the reopening had been put out of mind. The business had picked up a bit without it, but now was the time to get it going. Not just to keep her head above water, but to thrive.

Warmth flooded through Eleri at his words. She felt herself leaning closer to him, drawn in by the affection in his dark eyes. Her lips parted in anticipation and her pulse quickened.

Gareth reached out and eased a stray lock of hair away from her face, his fingers brushing against her cheek. "Eleri..." he murmured.

She could feel his breath, sweet with the scent of tea. Her eyes fluttered closed. This was it, the moment she realised they had both been waiting for.

His hand came up to cradle her jaw, tipping her face towards his. The surrounding bakery faded away. There was only Gareth, only this feeling of rightness as he bent his head towards hers.

At the first brush of his lips on hers, soft and tentative, Eleri felt a thrill shoot through her entire body. She leaned into him, desperate to eliminate any last sliver of space between them.

Gareth made an inaudible sound in his throat and pulled her tighter against him. The kiss deepened, their parted lips coming together again and again as months of unspoken emotion poured out.

A loud rap on the bakery's front window made them both jump. Eleri raised her eyes and noticed Mary pointing animatedly at the "Closed" sign, mouthing "Let me in!" through the glass.

With a rueful laugh, Eleri gave Gareth's hand a last squeeze before going to unlock the door for her chatty whirlwind of a friend. But all the while, her heart was pounding at the realisation of how close they had just come to crossing the line from friendship into something more. Eleri dabbed her lips, still feeling the ghost of Gareth's kiss there.

Chapter 8

Pale dawn light filtered through the linen curtains, falling across Eleri's face. She stirred, eyes blinking open to greet the morning. A smile spread across her face. Today was the big day!

Throwing back the duvet, she sprang out of bed and almost ran over to the window. She couldn't wait a moment longer. Eleri leaned out, gripping the sill, filling her lungs with fresh air. The crystal sky over Aberystwyth harbour promised perfect weather for the bakery's grand reopening.

Eleri twirled back to her room, unable to contain her excitement. She had so much to do to get ready before the big event! Humming a lilting Welsh tune, she plucked her favourite yellow dress from the wardrobe. As she washed and braided her hair, Eleri pictured dear Aunt Ffion bustling around the kitchen in just the same way, preparing for her own grand opening long ago.

The image of her Aunt Ffion as a nervous, excited girl on the bakery's first opening day filled Eleri's mind. She could just see Ffion flitting about, wisps of auburn hair escaping her braids as she whirled around the little kitchen. Hauling trays of steaming pastries from the oven, arranging them in the front display case. Wiping her dusty hands on her apron as she stepped outside to hang the fresh sign for "Ffwrn Ffion" as it was then before the rebranding.

Ffion would have taken a deep breath before unlocking the bakery door that first morning, just as Eleri did now. Across the years, Eleri felt so close to Aunt Ffion, even though she hadn't seen her as much as she would have liked. In this moment, she hoped she could do her proud.

Eleri gazed at her reflection in the old spotted mirror. "Wish me luck today, Aunt," she whispered. Ffion had scraped every penny to build her bakery up from nothing back then, pouring her dreams into her recipes. Now it was Eleri's turn to carry the torch. She was determined to make Ffion proud.

Downstairs, Eleri busied herself around the gleaming bakery, meticulously triple checking everything was ready. She peeked into the front display case, adjusting a tray of scones, so it sat just so. Stepping back, she inspected the array of pastries to ensure each raspberry tart and slices of bara brith were perfectly fanned out. Satisfied with the tempting spreads, she nodded briskly and smoothed her hands down her dress before moving to the next task.

In the kitchen, she opened the ovens one by one, leaning down to sniff each one, just in case. The sweet, yeasty aroma met her nose, untainted by even a whiff of burnt pastry. Good. Eleri continued her circuit of the kitchen, ensuring the granite countertops were prepped with ingredients and utensils to replenish stock throughout the busy day ahead. She imagined Aunt Ffion inspecting the kitchen with the same exacting eye generations ago on opening day. Everything must be flawless.

After one final survey, Eleri let out a breath. The gleaming bakery was ready and perfect for its grand reopening day. Satisfied all was in order, her gaze fell upon the small vase of daffodils she had placed on the counter in her aunt's memory. The bright yellow blooms were just perfect against the green walls. It would not have looked out of place in an interior design magazine cover.

"I won't let you down," Eleri promised, before returning to the doorway. She had just finished positioning the "Grand Reopening!" sign, with its jaunty bunting, in the bay window when the door chimed merrily.

"Bore da!" Gareth's warm smile lifted Eleri's spirits instantly. "Ready for the big day?"

"I think so." Eleri exhaled nervously, smoothing her dress. "I wanted everything perfect for the reopening. Aunt Ffion deserves that."

Gareth gave her shoulder a reassuring squeeze. "You deserve that. She'd be so proud of what you've accomplished here. Now try to relax and enjoy it!"

His calm confidence soothed Eleri's nerves. She was so thankful Gareth had offered to help with the preparations and mind the till during the rush.

Gareth and Eleri spent the next hour putting up the bunting and finishing the decorations, keeping the mood light with Gareth's banter.

The merry tinkle of the doorbell announced the first customers soon after they opened.

"Good morning!" Eleri warmly welcomed the familiar faces gazing around the cafe nostalgically. "Bore da!" she translated for her Welsh speaking customers.

As more locals filtered in, a cheerfulness suffused the bakery. Eleri chatted warmly with each familiar face, clasping their hands in greeting.

"Oh Eleri fach, it's so good to see this place open again," Mrs Williams said, squeezing Eleri's hand. "Your aunt would be happy for you, cariad."

Eleri smiled, a lump forming in her throat. "Thank you. That means the world to me."

Mr Pritchard ambled up, whistling with appreciation. "The place looks wonderful. You've done a fine job restoring it." He pressed a five-pound note into Eleri's palm with a wink. "A little something for luck on your big day."

"Mr Pritchard, you're too kind," Eleri protested with a chuckle, but Mr Pritchard insisted she take the note.

One after another, longtime customers shared memories about Aunt Ffion while slipping folded bills or coins into Eleri's hand "for luck." She clutched the unexpected bounty, overcome with gratitude for the outpouring of support on this special day.

Gareth breezed in, carrying the flour he'd popped out for, grinning broadly. "The place is buzzing already! What can I do to help?"

Eleri beamed back at him, her smile spreading from ear to

ear. She felt overwhelmed. Everything was coming together. She placed her hand on his arm.

"You're a gem. Could you help serve coffee and pastries?"

"With pleasure!" Gareth rolled up his sleeves, his brown eyes twinkling.

Eleri turned back to the growing crowd, fighting back happy tears. She shared laughter and hugs with longtime customers, many more wishing for her success. Their outpouring of support after the difficulties of the past few months filled Eleri with gratitude.

The cheerful warmth filling Aunt Ffion's bakery was shattered abruptly by the front door banging open with a violent crack. Patrons jumped in their seats as a dishevelled, unshaven man swaggered through the entrance, weaving. His bloodshot blue eyes were narrowed to slits, thin lips twisted in a sneer.

"Eleri!" he bellowed, voice slurring. "What the bloody hell do you think you're playing at?"

Eleri twisted to see the visitor, heartbeat stuttering, as all eyes swivelled between her and the drunken man. It was John. Why was he back?

John stumbled up to the counter, jabbing an accusing finger towards Eleri as patrons shrank back. "This pathetic little bakery has got no chance...you should've stayed with me. I'd have set you up proper."

Eleri trembled, paralysed by shock and anger, humiliated by this public confrontation. The carefree morning had shattered. She flinched as John sent a display of cupcakes crashing to the floor in his rage.

Just then, Gareth materialised at John's side, grasping his arm. "Come now, mate, I think it's time you left."

John shook him off violently, spittle flying from his lips. "Piss off! I'm not your mate. This has nothing to do with you!"

Unfazed, Gareth blocked his path to Eleri, broad shoulders squared. "The lady asked you to leave. Now."

With an incoherent roar, John launched himself at Gareth, who deftly sidestepped the blow. John hit the wooden table, doubling over with an oof, making the dishes rattle and cutlery scatter as Mr Pritchard rescued his cake from his outstretched arms. In a blur of movement, Gareth came up behind him, positioning John in an armlock. He propelled the flailing man towards the exit.

"Let go of me, you bloody tosser!" John sputtered furiously, but he was no match for Gareth's muscular strength. A few patrons hid grins at the spectacle.

The door slammed shut behind John's retreating back, leaving Eleri shaking. Adrenaline still buzzed through her veins after the ugly confrontation, but her hands trembled as her teacup rattled against the saucer.

Gareth was at her side in an instant. "All right, cariad?" His steady hands grasped her trembling ones.

Eleri nodded, not yet trusting her voice. She focused on taking slow, deep breaths to calm her racing heart. The bakery she had worked so hard to prepare now seemed chilled, the warmth leeched away by the hostile encounter.

"I'm okay," Eleri said finally, mustering a wan smile. "Just a bit unsettled."

Gareth's thumb brushed over her knuckles soothingly. The solid strength of his presence was comforting. But inwardly, Eleri still quaked from the confrontation. John's venom had rattled her, no matter how she tried to hide it. She focused on steadying her breathing, willing the shakes to cease. The way he had treated her in London... She didn't know he felt that way.

"I thought he didn't care. That last time, I thought just saying no would be enough."

"Oh Cariad, he's just hurting. Give him time." Gareth puts his arms around her, ignoring the curious eyes around them.

Eleri pulled back from Gareth's embrace. "I'm okay now. Bore da, everyone!" she called out brightly. "Who needs more coffee?"

Amidst the flurry of activity resuming, Mrs Pritchard patted Eleri's hand reassuringly.

"We always knew you were made of stern stuff, like your

Aunt Ffion. She'd be so proud of you, cariad."

Eleri squeezed her hand, thankful for her words. There were no secrets here, but there were advantages to that. With their support, she would make Ffion's bakery the heart of the community again.

***

John stumbled out of the bakery, fuming and cursing under his breath. That blasted woman! How dare she embarrass him in front of everyone! His hands formed tight fists by his sides.

Fury simmered as John turned the corner. He lashed out, boot striking an empty can. It skittered and clanged down the street.

Good. Let them hear. Let everyone know he wouldn't swallow this insult. Wouldn't let this humiliation go unanswered.

John's hands clenched, jaw tight. A storm raged beneath his stony expression. He welcomed the heat flooding his veins, burning away reason and restraint.

The can rolled to a stop, the echoing clatter fading. In the silence, John's breath sawed in and out, rage and vindication thrashing inside him. They had wounded his pride. He wouldn't let them get away with this!

John pictured Eleri's pretty face, probably laughing about him with her new boyfriend right now. Gareth, of all people. He'd known he'd held a candle for her all those years ago. But she'd chosen him, not Gareth. This could not be happening. The image made his blood boil. His steps quickened as he stomped down the pavement, teeth bared in a ferocious scowl

She would regret this, he vowed to himself. Leaving him behind to come running back here to play little bakery. Oh, he'd make sure she came to regret it.

As he turned the corner, still seeing red, he ploughed straight into a cheery blonde woman carrying a basket of muffins.

"Oi, watch it!" he barked, as a muffin tumbled to the pavement.

"So sorry! I can be a bit clumsy sometimes," the woman said brightly as she bent to retrieve the fallen muffin. Her voice was

63

soft, calming. Straightening her colourful skirt, she beamed up at him. "Hello John, long time, no see." At his blank expression, her face fell. "We had Mrs Evans together for maths. I'm Mary, remember?"

John scowled down at her. The sunlight glinting off her blonde hair made his head pound even more fiercely. But the muffins reminded him he was hungry.

"Say, you're looking peaky. Fancy a fresh blueberry muffin? I've got extras," Mary said, wafting the basket under his nose hopefully.

With a grunt, John accepted a muffin. It was fresh out of the oven, the blueberry bursting sweet and tangy on his tongue. Despite himself, he felt a bit soothed.

"Don't you remember me? From time to time, I lend a hand at Eleri's bakery. Not paid or anything. I just like helping her out," the woman continued cheerily as they walked. "Are you headed that way? I'm just popping by to drop off the muffins." She held it up like exhibit A in a court case.

At the mention of Eleri's name, John tensed, his hands clenching into fists. "No," he snarled through a mouthful of muffin. "I'm not going anywhere near that place."

Mary's eyes widened. "Oh dear. That was quite a scene you caused back there. But don't worry, Eleri's not one to hold grudges."

John froze, muscles coiling. This stranger had witnessed his outburst - the shouting, the wild gesturing, the cupcakes smashed in a fit of petty rage.

Mortification flooded through him, scalding his face. He averted his gaze, unable to meet the woman's eyes, to see the judgement and disgust that must fill them.

John dug his nails into his palms, willing himself not to flee in cowardice. He had to face the consequences of his pathetic lack of control. Had to own this moment of weakness laid bare before a total stranger.

"Yeah, well, she deserved it, the way she ditched me to come running back here," he muttered, shoving his hands in his pockets.

Mary touched his arm with a light touch. "Breakups are so hard. But we all deserve to find happiness. I'm sure you will too, someday."

John stared at the pavement, unable to meet her eyes. She had seen him at his worst, raging like a spoiled child. Ugly shame curdled in his gut. He scuffed his shoe against the curb, jaw clenched.

With Mary's soothing presence beside him, the red haze of anger and wounded pride seeped away, leaving only regret and embarrassment over his outburst. He wasn't the man he wanted to be, but here, at least, was someone who still believed he could change. Her guileless blue eyes were so sincere it disarmed him.

Mary tilted her head towards the street ahead. "I should get back to the bakery to help Eleri and Gareth close up. But you're welcome to join me, if you'd like to apologise to her."

John shuffled his feet, staring down at the pavement. "I shouldn't have gone off like that," he admitted gruffly. "But I doubt she wants to see me again so soon."

"Oh, I wouldn't be so sure," Mary said, an optimistic smile crinkling her eyes. "Eleri has always been very forgiving. And who can stay angry after one of her famous blueberry muffins?"

Despite himself, John felt the tension in his shoulders ease a bit. Maybe he could salvage a scrap of dignity after all. But confronting Eleri again so soon would be too much.

"Alright, maybe... Just not quite yet," he conceded. "But will you have a drink with me first? I could use some friendly company."

Mary checked her watch, then smiled up at him again. "I suppose the bakery can spare me for a bit. Lead the way!"

As they walked down the street together, Mary chattering, John felt his anxiety dissipating. Her guileless friendliness was oddly soothing.

When she stumbled on the uneven pavement, almost dropping the muffin basket, he reflexively put a hand out to steady her.

"Whoops! Saved them just in time," Mary said with a grin. Despite himself, John felt the corners of his mouth quirk upward in response. It was the first time he could remember smiling all day.

They settled onto barstools at the pub. As John swallowed the first sip of bitter ale, he let out a long exhale, feeling muscles unknot he hadn't realised were clenched tight.

Mary smiled kindly as she sipped her ginger ale. "Rough day, eh? But tomorrow's a new day."

John nodded, the dark cloud over his mind lifting. With Mary's calming presence beside him, the future seemed hopeful. She'd just seen the worst of him, and she was still here. He rolled his stiff shoulders, feeling the tension drain away.

"You know, I always thought you seemed like a decent guy," Mary said, putting her basket down. "What happened between you and Eleri? If you don't mind talking about it, that is."

John stared down at the worn wood of the bar. What had happened? He remembered the dizzy infatuation at university. How proud he'd felt to have the popular, pretty girl on his arm. But the initial thrill had faded over the years into a dull resentment as she focused more on her baking than on him. He'd tried to convince her to give up her silly bakery dreams. There was no way they could afford to set up a business in London and keep their standard of living. Until eventually, her aunt died, and she inherited that blasted bakery from her. She'd refused to stay, saying Aberystwyth was her home.

"I guess we wanted different things," he said finally, taking a long swallow of bitter ale. "I wanted her with me, but she wanted to come back here."

Mary nodded sympathetically. "It hurts to realise you're growing apart. But sometimes love just runs its course." She smiled a bit sadly. "Like Gareth and me back in school."

John's head jerked up in surprise. "You and Gareth? But he's so..."

"Serious? Bookish?" Mary laughed. "Opposites attract, or so they say. We were young, it didn't last. But we've stayed friends."

John absorbed this quietly. He'd never imagined Gareth had a history with someone like Mary. It made him seem less intimidating somehow. More human.

"Do you think..." He hesitated. "Do you think Eleri and I could ever be friends again?"

Mary beamed at him. "Of course! It might take some time, but I know she misses you too, in her own way."

John felt a small spark of hope amidst the ashes of his anger. With Mary's warmth beside him, the future seemed a little brighter.

"What do you say we head over to the bakery now?" Mary suggested. "I'll be with you the whole time. Start with helping to tidy up - a peace offering, then see what happens?"

The fight drained from John, leaving him weary. Mary's gentle compassion had chipped away at his icy bitterness, kindling a fragile wish for reconciliation.

He knew further outbursts would gain nothing. There was no honour in petty revenge or wounded pride. If any shred of dignity remained, it was time to grasp it before he was too far gone.

John took a deep breath, steadying his nerves. The road ahead would be difficult, requiring humility and patience— traits he lacked. But for the first time, he felt ready to try.

It was time to stop making excuses. To stand up and take responsibility. To face the pain and anger head-on, without lashing out or assigning blame. No more tantrums.

Resolved, John straightened his shoulders. The future waited to be rebuilt.

John faltered as he and Mary approached the familiar bakery storefront. Apprehension and doubt almost made him turn back. What if Eleri rejected his attempt at an apology?

But Mary touched his arm. "It will be alright, you'll see. One day at a time."

Bolstered by her support, John squared his shoulders and walked through the cheery door chime. Inside, he hesitated, scuffing his toe against the polished wood floor.

"Hello John."

Eleri stood waiting, face unreadable. John stuck his hands in his pockets to hide their trembling. "Eleri, I... I'm sorry for the way I behaved earlier," he said, voice cracking. "It was out of order."

He held his breath, shoulders hunched, as he awaited her verdict.

***

Eleri sank into the worn armchair at the back of the cafe as the last patron slipped out the door, barely stifling a yawn. Bone-deep exhaustion seeped through her body after the long but rewarding first day of the rest of her life. She grinned. She loved a good cliche. Her eyes closed, and she leaned into Gareth's sturdy shoulder as he perched on the chair's arm.

"Quite a day, eh, cariad?" he murmured, voice resonating in his chest beneath her ear. His large, calloused hand engulfed hers.

"I'm completely knackered," she admitted with a tired chuckle, Welsh lilt warming her words. "But so thrilled the bakery's off to a good start, thanks to you."

Gareth pressed a kiss into her waves of auburn hair, the faint scent of rosewater filling his nose. "Wild horses couldn't have kept me from helping you today."

Eleri smiled, heart swelling with gratitude for this kind, steadfast man who had come into her life just when she'd needed him most.

The cheery chime of the doorbell jarred Eleri from her comfortable respite. She stiffened, nerves jangling again until she saw it was only Mary, wispy flyaway blond curls framing her round, rosy-cheeked face.

"Mary fach! So good of you to come help close up." Eleri embraced her friend's soft, pillowy frame. A distracted thought fitted across her mind. Had her friend lost weight?

"Of course, Leri! And I brought someone along to have a chat with you if that's alright." Mary's eyes glinted knowingly as she glanced behind her.

Eleri's mouth fell open in surprise as John's tall, lanky figure hovered uncertainly in the doorway, eyes downcast beneath his ash-blond fringe.

Gareth tensed next to Eleri, his jovial mood evaporating. She gave his hand a warning squeeze before standing to face John.

"Hello, John." Her voice came out steady, betraying none of the rolling emotions within her. This man had hurt her, but she saw only pain and regret in the lines of his face now. She would hear him out.

Eleri studied John's downcast face, seeing the regret in his eyes. Her heart softened, despite the lingering sting of his cruel words.

"Thank you for apologising, John. That couldn't have been easy," she said. "I appreciate you making the effort."

John looked up, tentative hope dawning in his expression. "I shouldn't have said those things. I was angry, but that's no excuse."

"You're right, it still hurts. But I understand how painful breakups can be." Eleri glanced at Gareth as if for reassurance. "I'm willing to forgive and move forward, if you are."

"I'd like that," John said, a bit gruffly. "I know I've got some changes to make, but it helps to know you don't hate me."

Eleri smiled. "I could never hate you, John. We shared a lot together." She hesitated, then asked, "Would you like to stay for some tea and cake? I baked your favourite chocolate gateau."

John's face lit up in a crooked grin. "I'd love that. Thanks, Eleri."

As John devoured an enormous slice of chocolate gateau, the knots in Eleri's chest loosened. With Mary's encouragement, she felt certain John would find his way again. And she had all she needed right here.

Gareth slipped his hand into hers, giving a supportive squeeze. No matter what storms blew through, the roots she'd put down here would hold fast.

Chapter 9

The crunch of glass under Gareth's boots sounded deafening in the early morning hush. He paused on the pavement, glancing first at the 'Closed' sign hanging askew in the door. Then his eyes lifted to the shattered front window of his antique shop, his stomach sinking at the destruction.

Spider webbed cracks radiated out from a gaping hole in the centre of the large pane, giving it the look of a broken mirror. Jagged shards clung precariously to the edges of the frame like broken teeth, while mounds of debris lay strewn across the doorstep glinting sharply. The sharp tang of rainwater mixed with old varnish hung in the air.

Gareth hesitated, listening for any sound of an intruder still inside. Only silence greeted him, punctuated by the occasional clink of glass dropping free. He stepped closer with caution, wincing as the glass crunched under his boots. He scanned the chaotic scene, taking in the heaps of wreckage threatening to slice through his soles if he wasn't careful. What a mess... and what a way to start the morning.

Crouching down, Gareth selected a larger chunk, turning it over in his fingers. The fracturing along the edges spoke of something heavy striking the window at force. He noted the point of impact was chest height for an average man. This was no accidental damage or stray ball. Someone had deliberately smashed the windowpane with malicious intent.

Gareth's jaw clenched, his mind flashing back to the previous day. Eleri's smiling face as she served her customers at her bakery's reopening. The hearty applause and cheerful laughter ringing out from her friends gathered in support. Then the drunken shout that cut through the merriment, John lurching through the crowd, ranting and unsteady.

His blood ran cold. Surely John wouldn't have...

No. But as much as he wanted to deny it, Gareth knew in his gut the drunkard was behind this vandalism. Who else had such a petty grudge against him? It must be retaliation for the public shame of getting tossed from the bakery opening. Gareth cursed under his breath. He should have known better than to hope John would just walk away quietly. Men like him clung to their anger and spite.

Gareth's shoulders slumped as he rocked back on his heels among the wreckage. This was no random act by bored teenagers. No, he could almost picture John out here in the dark early hours, drunk with rage and whiskey as he hurled the stone with vicious force. The spiderweb of cracks radiating out from the chest-high impact seemed to scream the vindictiveness of the act. John had singled out the main shop window, wanting to inflict maximum damage. A childish effort to soothe his wounded ego by targeting Gareth's livelihood.

With a weary sigh, Gareth rose and tested the shop door. Unlocked. He'd forgotten to lock it last night among all the excitement. The irony stung, leaving a doorway gaping open beside the shattered windowpane. He hesitated on the threshold, part of him afraid to see what state the interior was in after last night's storm. But he couldn't put it off. Steeling himself, Gareth stepped inside.

The crunch and crackle of glass underfoot continued as he moved further in, the sound setting his nerves on edge. Low morning light filtered through the window, remnants threw rainbow-hued patterns across the floorboards and walls, strangely beautiful against the ravages of destruction. The air held the tang of old varnish mixed with rainwater and wood rot.

His heart sank at the pools still trickling through the floor planks from the night's downpour. The rug just inside the window would be ruined if it stayed soaked. Hurrying over, Gareth rolled up the sodden rug, grimacing as water sloshed over his shoes. He'd have to check if any of his shelves or cabinets closer to the window had suffered water damage, too. The storm had certainly made a chaotic situation even worse.

Leaning the wet rug against the wall to deal with later, Gareth grabbed a broom and dustpan from the back room. He had no choice but to start the cleanup process now, as much as it pained him. This place was his passion, filled with treasures and memories accumulated over the years. To see it violated by John's petty retaliation cut deeply. As Gareth swept the sea of broken glass into piles, bitterness threatened to settle in his heart.

But he refused it purchase. No, John may have meant this vandalism to crush Gareth's spirit, but he would fail. Gareth had weathered worse storms before, though rarely so literal, he thought wryly. He would simply board up the window for now, file a claim, contact his insurance agent to start repairs...

Gareth's spiralling thoughts stuttered to a halt. Insurance. Repairs. Costs. Sweeping a hand roughly through his hair, he cursed again, louder this time. Money had been tight at the antique shop as of late, what with the expanding supermarkets drawing away foot traffic to the other side of town. His savings were almost gone from keeping the place afloat over the past few months. Now this damage would set him back even further.

Closing his eyes, he could see flames licking the walls, turning his beloved antique shop into a blackened husk. The acrid smell of smoke filled his lungs. He opened his eyes with a gasp. Just a vision. But it had felt so real.

Gareth blinked, the actual shop coming back into focus. The stress was getting to him, conjuring worst-case scenarios in his mind. He rubbed his eyes wearily.

For now, at least, it was just a broken window and some minor water damage. Manageable issues he could mop up and repair. But the vivid vision lingered, a chilling premonition of what could come to pass if his fortunes didn't improve.

Gareth squared his shoulders with resolve. He wouldn't let that nightmare future come to be. This shop was his whole life. He had to keep fighting, no matter how bleak things seemed. With determination, he grabbed a brush and got to work fixing what he could.

As Gareth aggressively shoved more wreckage into the dustpan, waves of frustration and despair washed over him. How much more could he withstand before losing his dream entirely? This latest hit was testing his endurance to the limit. He wanted to scream at the injustice of it all.

His phone chimed with a new alert - just another payday loan app promising fast cash in times of need. Gareth's jaw tightened. He had sworn off those predators after barely scraping his way out from under a mountain of debt last time. How did they even know? But as he took in the shop's gutted interior - the glass window reduced to shards, merchandise scattered across the floor now slick with rain water - desperation mounted. Gareth's hands shook as he lugged a dustpan of broken glass to the bin, his breaths coming faster. This little shop was all he had left after the divorce ripped his world apart, his last chance at maintaining a stable income. But repairs would cost more than he could scrape together in months. His stomach twisted, heartbeat pounding in his ears as he considered the unthinkable. Before common sense could intervene, Gareth grabbed his phone with trembling fingers. He knew it was reckless. One more step toward financial ruin. But the cash would be in his account now when he needed it most. Hardly daring to breathe, pulse racing, he opened the predator's app and typed in a request for £500, providing his account details with a wince. Seconds later, the transfer was approved, funds appearing instantly. Gareth slumped against the counter, shame and relief swirling within him. It was a desperate choice, but if his livelihood had any hope of surviving, it had been a necessary one.

At least the insurance would help cover the cost of repairs when it eventually came through. He'd have to close the shop for a week or so. Hardly ideal timing, with summer tourist season underway. His face brightened. At least he could give the whole place a touch up with paint with the loan. Brighten it up a bit, make it more enticing. It had worked for the bakery. Maybe he should take up his own advice.

Gareth's thoughts returned to John. They had been friends years ago. How had he changed so much? He'd airways been obstinate, prone to grudges, petty, but Gareth naively hoped he'd get the hint. Clearly not. This vandalism was just the pathetic man's way of salvaging his bruised ego.

The bell above the door jingled merrily as Eleri entered, holding two steaming mugs of coffee. She stopped short in the doorway, her emerald eyes growing round as pennies at the destruction before her.

"Bore da, what happened here?" she asked.

Gareth gave her a weary smile. "Just a bit of bad luck, I reckon." He pushed a mound of glass into a pile. "I reckon it had to be John."

Eleri pursed her lips, displeased, but unsurprised by her ex's antics.

"That bloody idiot. I'm so sorry, cariad. I honestly thought when he said sorry, that would be the end." She set the coffees down with a clatter and grabbed another broom to help with the cleanup.

They worked in companionable silence for a few minutes before Gareth spoke up again.

"I'll have to shut the shop while this mess gets sorted. The timing's not ideal, what with profits being down and all."

"With the tourist crowds coming, we could make this bad news into some good news," Eleri said, her eyes lighting up.

"I'm all ears if you've got a plan, cariad," Gareth said, leaning on his broom.

"What if you sold some of your antiques and collectibles at the bakery while you're closed for repairs?" Eleri suggested eagerly. "We could set up nice displays, make an inviting little shop to pull in customers."

Gareth rubbed his chin thoughtfully. "You know, that just might work. The exposure would be good for both of us."

"It's settled then," Eleri said, clapping her hands decisively.

"We'll take this smashed window and turn it into an opportunity. Oh, it would be brilliant! I'd be happy to help set up a little shop for you." She waved her arms out expansively. "Ooh, just imagine it - we could decorate with your pictures, furniture, maybe put out some free samples of pastries to get people interested!"

Her green eyes were bright with enthusiasm as she gestured animatedly, thrilled at the thought of helping Gareth in his time of need, as he had helped her.

As they finished cleaning up the glass, Gareth watched Eleri subtly, noticing the way the morning sun lit up her auburn hair and made her green eyes sparkle. He admired the cute way she scrunched up her nose while sweeping, and the methodical way she moved through the tasks at hand. His eyes traced the outline of her profile, feeling a swell of gratitude for this remarkable woman.

Ever since she'd got back, she had become such a bright spot in his life. Supporting each other through respective hard times, their friendship had blossomed into something deeper over the past months. And now here she was again, quick to offer help when he needed it most.

With the floor now clear of debris, Gareth grabbed a spare piece of plywood and some tools from the basement. Together, they boarded up the broken window temporarily.

"I'll give Mary a ring and see if she can help us move some of your antiques over," Eleri said, a cheerful lilt in her voice.

"Thank you so much for offering to display them at the cafe, Eleri."

She nodded. On impulse, he pulled her into a quick but fierce hug.

"Thank you, cariad. Don't know what I'd do without you."

She leaned into the embrace for a moment before pulling back, cheeks flushed. Clearing her throat, she collected the now-cold mugs of coffee and headed for the door.

"I'll text you as soon as Mary can help. Chin up, we'll get through this."

With a final dazzling smile and a cheery "hwyl fawr," she

pushed out the door, setting the bells jingling again.

Gareth watched her go, an odd mixture of feelings swirling through him. Gratitude, admiration, and something deeper he couldn't quite name. All he knew for certain was that Eleri Rhys had become indispensable in his life. And he would do whatever it took to support her happiness in return.

John's petty retaliation would not get the better of them. Together, they would take this misfortune and transform it into something good.

Chapter 10

The sweet scent of baking bread enveloped Eleri as she slid the last plump loaf into the bakery's display case. Morning sunlight angled through the windows, illuminating the empty cafe's polished wood floors and tables. Eleri treasured these solitary mornings alone with her baking, when it felt like she could sense Aunt Ffion's presence most strongly. She felt that fulfilling her aunt's wishes to scatter her ashes had gained her approval, but she also felt an undercurrent of annoyance, disappointment, and fear for her. Her abilities were never that reliable, but she couldn't shake those feelings. Eleri's hands worked rhythmically, kneading and shaping dough with flour-dusted fingers. The familiar motions calmed her. She could almost feel Aunt Ffion beside her, guiding her hands through the steps they'd done together countless times.

As Eleri rinsed the sticky residue from her hands, the warmth of the kitchen vanished in an instant. She shuddered as an icy chill slithered down her spine. Glancing up, she gasped, nearly dropping the ceramic bowl with a clatter.

Ffion's pale, translucent form stood before her, more solid than any vision before. Eleri's heart pounded against her ribs. She opened her mouth, but no words emerged. Ffion lifted a slender hand, eyes grave beneath her wispy hair.

"Trouble comes that could ruin all you've built," she warned, voice hollow as if from another world. "Time is running out, Eleri."

Eleri gave a silent shake of her head, feeling perplexed and frightened.

Ffion's blurred outline leaned closer. "Don't take anything at face value. Keep your guard up. Not everything is as it seems. Don't trust what you see until you know everything." Her voice faded on the last word.

"What do you mean?" Eleri finally managed, but Ffion only repeated her warning before dissolving into empty air.

Eleri stood frozen for a long moment, pulse racing as she struggled to understand the bizarre encounter. Her aunt's spirit had always been a comforting presence in the bakery. But this... this felt different. The grave warning left Eleri rattled, a sense of foreboding settling heavily on her shoulders. She wrapped her arms around herself, shoulders hunched against a sudden cold that penetrated to her bones. Something was very wrong.

Eleri's mind swirled with unanswered questions, but she pushed them aside for later. Right now, she needed Gareth's steadying presence and reassuring voice more than anything. The icy chill still clung to her bones, making her shiver. She had to tell him about Aunt Ffion's bizarre warning. Surely Gareth could help unravel its cryptic meaning, she told herself.

Moving in a daze, she closed up the bakery, the cheery "Open" sign flipped abruptly to "Closed". She hurried through the rainy streets of Aberystwyth, her boots splashing through puddles as she made her way to Gareth's antique shop on the seafront.

Eleri sank into a chair in Gareth's flat above his shop, pressing a hand to her pounding heart.

She recounted the details in a rush - the icy chill, Ffion's sudden spectral appearance, the ominous message about dark forces and deception. Gareth listened intently, his expression growing serious.

"Why haven't you told me anything about this before?"

"She only appeared this morning." Eleri replied, confused.

"No hearing voices. You didn't tell me you were psychic. When you found the locket, that would have been the perfect time to tell me."

"Well, yes, but it's not something you just blurt out. You might think I was crazy."

Gareth sank back in his chair, crossing his legs.

"You know, this could be related to the locket you found. Maybe that's what it does, helps you to stop the spirits."

"It's not doing a bang-up job so far. It all felt so real," Eleri whispered when she had finished.

Gareth hesitated, polishing a vintage pocket watch. He had always been pragmatic to a fault, slow to trust anything without tangible evidence. He'd obsessed about the local legends, but he didn't really believe it. Confronted with the possibility that ghosts could be real was unnerving. But seeing Eleri so shaken stirred an innate need to comfort and protect.

"I believe you," he said finally. "Whatever happened, it's clearly left you rattled. We'll sort this out, I promise."

He set the watch down and came around the table to sit beside her. The familiar warmth of his presence was soothing, easing some of Eleri's frayed nerves.

His steadfast support eased her frayed nerves. Gareth suggested Ffion's warning might relate to the old legends of vengeful spirits haunting Aberystwyth. "I told you about the lockets legend, but there are others. Maybe the ghosts are attracted to you."

Eleri nodded, considering the plausibility of darker forces lurking beneath the town's peaceful veneer. She leaned into Gareth's comforting embrace, drawing courage from his strength.

"We'll face this together," he promised.

Later that evening, Gareth walked Eleri home through misty streets. Despite lingering unease, her earlier terror had faded. Gareth's stalwart presence gave her hope.

At her door, he squeezed her shoulder. "Get some rest. We'll start unravelling this mystery soon."

Eleri watched him disappear into the fog, filled with gratitude. Come what may, Gareth would stand with her against the darkness.

That night as Eleri prepared for bed, Eleri's gaze snagged on an old, framed photograph of her and Aunt Ffion. She froze. There, reflected in the glass over the photo, was the shadowy figure of a weeping woman hovering behind her. Eleri gasped and spun around, but there was nothing there. The ghostly woman had vanished.

Trembling, she glanced back at the photo. This time, only her own pale face stared back. "I must be seeing things," Eleri muttered, rubbing her tired eyes.

Eleri got into bed, images of Aunt Ffion still fresh in her mind. As she drifted off to sleep, she thought she heard faint crying.

The next morning, Eleri awoke feeling unrested. As she went about her day, she couldn't shake the uneasy feeling that she was being watched. Every time she glanced in the mirror, she expected to see the ghostly figure again, but saw nothing.

That night, as Eleri got ready for bed, her eyes again fell upon the photo of her and Aunt Ffion. She smiled sadly at the memory. Just then, the photo slipped from its place and crashed to the floor. Eleri jumped at the sound. When she picked up the photo, the glass was cracked right between her face and Aunt Ffion's.

Eleri shuddered, feeling freezing and terrified.

Chapter 11

Gareth meandered through the labyrinth of bookcases and curios in his basement from when the antique shop had belonged to his grandfather. For weeks, Eleri had confided in him about a spectre haunting her—not only her aunt Ffion, but a weeping woman disturbing her dreams and glimpsed in shadows. Gareth hated seeing Eleri so distressed, so he delved into the shop's archives, seeking anything that might explain this phantom.

He methodically worked through the oldest boxes first. The place most likely to house the older books and objects. His grandfather's plans to create his own museum lay in these boxes before he died unexpectedly. Gareth's back strained and arms ached under the weight as he brought each one down to create new piles of sorted town history. Dust and mildew filled the air, making him cough every time he opened a fresh box.

Squinting in a dim corner, he crouched down to inspect a promising box of dust-covered volumes. He smiled as he remembered playing hide and seek as a child. The boxes were stacked precariously over him, towering against the old brick walls. He shuddered to think what would have happened if they had fallen on him.

Rifling through mildewed pages, he caught a glint of gold embossing on an ancient leather binding. Gingerly, he extracted the heavy tome, causing a plume of dust to fill the air that made him cough. As it cleared, Gareth discerned ornate calligraphy filling the timeworn pages. Intricate illuminations depicted medieval scenes of knights and ladies. He turned each fragile leaf, scrutinising for anything related to ghosts, spirits, or mysticism.

Towards the back of the book, an illuminated image captured Gareth's attention. It depicted a regal man with jet black hair falling to his shoulders. The man had chiselled features, wearing fine clothes showing him to be noble. At his side stood an elegant woman with cascading red-gold hair that glowed likes rays of sunlight. Around both their necks hung twin lockets made from burnished silver, covered with intricate Celtic knot designs.

Gareth leaned closer, transfixed. There was something hauntingly familiar about those matching pendants. As he studied the stylised patterns, recognition sparked. Those concentric circles... the delicate angled lines... his hand twitched as he remembered tracing the locket's imprint, seared into his memory.

"It can't be..." he murmured. But the more he scrutinised the antique painting, the more certain he became. That was the same locket that had become legend—and now, they were in his and Eleri's lives. Gareth's breath caught as the implications sunk in. There were two matching cursed lockets, not one.

Under the elaborate painting, the names of Amelia and Cadwgan shone up from the ancient page inscribed in gold paint.

He pored over the obscure Welsh text surrounding the illustration, struggling to decipher the archaic vocabulary. As meaning emerged, his eyes went wide. This was no ordinary story, but a tragic legend of two ill-fated souls in medieval Wales—a Welsh lord named Cadwgan and his English lady, Amelia. Forbidden love between a nobleman and commoner. Forbidden by the historical divide between their cultures. He read on. They secretly exchanged antique lockets as tokens of their eternal bond, believing their love transcended social rules and national enmity, but his family made sure they could not be together. This was an older version of the legend he already knew about - but the two lockets were different. The illustration was beautiful, vivid blues, gold and oranges. His finger brushed the page. They must have cost a fortune. His eyes were drawn back to the text.

The legend took a darker turn. Gareth decoded phrases about a "curse" and "fate" that befell the star-crossed lovers. Cadwgan married a noblewoman of the south. Endless grief and longing stained the lockets thereafter. Gareth's pulse quickened. Could these be the source of the spectre haunting Eleri's dreams?

Clutching the leather-bound tome to his chest, Gareth rushed from the dusty basement, nearly stumbling in his haste to share these revelations with Eleri herself. He burst into sunlight, the sea breeze ruffling his dark hair as he jogged down Aberystwyth's streets toward her bakery café.

He weaved between overflowing flower boxes erupting in vivid purple and yellow blooms, the last of summer's bounty before autumn crept in. The hearty scent of lavender mingled with the salty whiff of the nearby harbour. Up ahead, the heavenly aroma of freshly baked bread and brewing coffee signified he was getting close.

Rounding the corner, he spotted Eleri's cheerful blue cafe, tables dotted outside with the last loyal customers of the season. The door chimes tinkled merrily as he crossed the threshold into the warm interior.

"Bore da, Eleri fach!" blinking as his eyes adjusted from sunny streets to the interior bathed in warm light.

Eleri looked up from the espresso machine, her emerald eyes lighting up. "Gareth! What a lovely surprise."

He lifted the ancient tome. "I've found something— something about that ghost."

Intrigue flashed across Eleri's delicate features. She glanced at her friend Mary, who smiled and shooed Eleri away from the counter. "Go on, I'll watch the shop. This sounds fascinating!"

Gareth led Eleri to a table by the window, dappled with sunbeams. He opened the manuscript to the illuminated lovers.

"I discovered this in my grandfather's collection. It's very old, and it mentions two medieval lovers who wore these lockets." He indicated the intricate pendants around their necks. "But their love was cursed. They were split up by his family and he was forced to marry another. He died the next year of grief."

Eleri's emerald eyes widened as she studied the intricate

illustration. Her fingers hovered over the ancient pages, almost afraid to touch the lovers frozen in time. Her graceful neck tilted thoughtfully, auburn waves spilling over one shoulder.

"Cursed love, fate..." she murmured. Her delicate brows drew together, and she bit her bottom lip as if fighting back emotion. Slim hands gripped her cup tightly.

After a moment, she lifted her gaze to meet Gareth's, determination burning behind the sheen of tears. "You're right, there must be a connection to the spirit haunting me. These lockets are key." She nodded firmly, steeling herself. "We must search for the second one. For Amelia... and for me."

Gareth nodded. "I know it seems unlikely. But the dreams started when you came back here. There must be a connection." He hesitated before adding, "I want to help uncover the truth about this spirit. You shouldn't have to face this alone."

Eleri gave him a small but grateful smile. "She has red hair, too. If they never married, how can she be my ancestor?"

Gareth grabbed the book and flipped through the pages. "Here. She was banished and pregnant. He never knew."

Eleri sat back, expelling a sharp breath. "Thank you, Gareth. I appreciate you searching for answers." She bit her lip, gazing at the lovers frozen in time. "Perhaps the ghost is this Amelia, longing for her lost love? And something about this place, my return... woke her spirit?"

"My thoughts exactly," Gareth agreed, hope rising that they were on the right path. "We have to find the second locket. They're the key to understanding this curse, and hopefully lay Amelia's spirit to rest."

Eleri met his eyes, resolve hardening her delicate features. "Let's do it. If the lockets are here in Aberystwyth, we'll find them."

***

John sat in one of the comfy chairs at the back corner of Eleri's bakery, sipping his coffee while half-listening to the chatter of other patrons. His eyes kept drifting to the sun-kissed auburn hair and willowy frame of his ex-girlfriend across the room.

After months apart, just being near Eleri made him ache with regret.

He had taken her for granted when they were together. Letting her end it and move back to Aberystwyth was the biggest mistake of his life. Now John wanted to win her back, but he was conflicted. Mary's blue eyes seemed to superimpose on hers wherever he thought of Eleri. He only came in when Mary was around. He'd heard what happened to Gareth's shop, and he knew he would be blamed, even though he'd been in Borth that night. Mary had a way of diffusing situations.

As he brooded, movement at Eleri's corner table caught his eye. She was seated with Gareth, heads bent over some old book. John sank lower in his chair, angling himself behind a large potted fern to avoid being spotted. He leaned forward, straining to overhear the hushed conversation from Eleri's corner table.

His leg jittered under the table as he pressed his ear closer, picking up snippets about "lockets" and "fate." John's eyes narrowed, his shoulders tensing. His fingers drummed an agitated beat on his mug handle.

Noticing Mary's gaze drift his way, John feigned a relaxed posture and took a casual sip of coffee. But his attention remained fixed on the intriguing exchange. He caught them mentioning ancestors.

John's jaw clenched at the implication. Were they plotting to cheat him out of what was rightfully his? He wouldn't let them pull one over on him... His pulse quickened as he devised his own plan. This time, he wouldn't let Eleri slip away so easily.

"I'm certain they're the same cursed lockets haunting us," Gareth said, pointing at an illustration.

Locket? John's interest sharpened. The only locket he knew of was the one belonging to Eleri's late Aunt Ffion he'd seen her wearing once. Eleri must have inherited it when her aunt died along with this bakery.

Were these two plotting to find that locket and steal his rightful inheritance? John's jaw clenched at the thought. After supporting Eleri financially all those years, he deserved a share of anything she gained. After all, they'd been common in law husband and wife even if they hadn't married. He ignored the faint whisper in the recesses of his mind, asking whose fault was that.

He watched the pair grow more animated as they kept mentioning "the lockets" and a "curse." John had heard enough. He strode over to their table, forcing a smile.

"Well, well, sorry to intrude on this intimate twosome."

Eleri looked up, surprise flashing in her emerald eyes. "John! I thought you were at work this morning?"

"Got it all handled early, so I thought I'd pop in. But clearly I'm interrupting something." He gave a pointed look at the old book.

Gareth bristled. "Just discussing some old local legends. We'll have to continue another time, Eleri. See you later." He clasped her hand before departing with the book.

John slid into the vacant chair. "Local legends, eh? Looked more like treasure hunting plans to me." He lowered his voice. "Come now, Eleri, we know each other too well for secrets. Are you and lover boy tracking down your inheritance?"

Eleri frowned. "Inheritance? What are you implying?"

"Don't play coy. I heard you two plotting about lockets." John leaned forward. "We both know that means your Aunt Ffion's antique locket. The one you inherited."

Eleri's eyes flashed. "You were eavesdropping? And made wild assumptions? How dare you!" She stood up, her chair scraping against the floor. "I think you should leave now, John."

John stayed seated, glaring up at her. "Not until you admit you and Gareth are scheming to find that locket, so you can sell it. And after all, we meant to each other, I deserve a share of the profits."

Eleri looked utterly flabbergasted. But before she could respond, Gareth reappeared and grasped John's shoulder in a firm grip.

"I believe the lady asked you to go," he said through gritted teeth.

John shook off Gareth's hand and stood. "This is between me and Eleri. Stay out of it."

Gareth moved to stand closer to Eleri. "From what I heard, you were rudely making accusations and demands. Leave. Now." His brown eyes bored into John.

John stood tall, tilting his chin up defiantly.

"I'm not leaving without what I deserve," John said, steel in his tone. He planted his feet firmly, squaring his shoulders.

"You have no right to make demands," Gareth said, muscles taut like a spring.

John met his glare and leaned in closer, unfazed by their height difference. "I have every right. Eleri owes me." He crossed his arms over his chest, looking Gareth up and down dismissively. "Back off, little man. This is between me and her."

John kept his body loose but ready, in case this turned physical. He wouldn't be caught off guard. He didn't scare easily. Especially not by the likes of Gareth.

"Not without what I deserve. Half that locket's value belongs to me!" He repeated.

In a blur, Gareth grabbed John by the shirtfront and spun him around, marching him to the door. John struggled in fury and embarrassment.

"Get your hands off me! You're both going to regret this!" John yelled.

Gareth firmly shoved him out onto the pavement. "The only thing I regret is not doing that sooner. Stay away from Eleri or we will have words again."

He slammed the door.

John's face burned as he dusted himself off. His hands shook with the urge to hit something. Gareth would pay for this humiliation.

Storming down the street, John's pulse pounded in his ears. He dug his fingernails into his palms, barely noticing the stinging crescents they left behind. All he could see was Gareth's smug face as he tossed him out like the rubbish - again.

John kicked a bin violently. It boomed but held fast, startling a flock of seagulls into flight. He wished he could do the same to Gareth.

Passing pedestrians gave John a wide berth as he stomped onward, muttering curses to himself. His mind churned with vengeance. He had to get that locket first. Then Gareth and Eleri would be the ones apologising.

Fine, if they refused him his rightful due, he would have to take matters into his own hands. John stormed off hatching plans to follow them and find out everything about the locket. He would prove they owed him.

His thoughts flashed back to their London flat years ago. John had just started his new accountancy job, eager to prove he could support them both. But Eleri dreamed bigger.

"I want to open my own bakery, John," she had said, eyes bright with ambition. "I found the perfect little storefront in Camden. We could turn it into an adorable cafe."

John shook his head, fresh out of university and overwhelmed with his new workload. "I'm not sure we can swing that rent on my salary, love. Give it some time."

"But I can help pay for it by working there myself," Eleri pressed eagerly.

"It's too risky," John insisted. "Better stay practical for now. I don't want you worrying over finances if the business fails."

Despite her pleas, he refused to budge. He knew the sensible choice was to wait until they were more secure. So Eleri reluctantly shelved her dreams, not wanting to overburden John as he tried establishing his new career.

Over the years, he had supported them in London on his modest accountant's income. He thought Eleri was happy enough, even without having her own bakery. Now, to see her embracing that dream with Gareth's help cut John deeply.

After all he had sacrificed, how could she throw it all away? Half of whatever profits she made were rightfully his. John's face hardened with cold resolve. He would prove it, no matter what it took. This time, he refused to lose Eleri again.

Chapter 12

The sea air ruffled Mary's blonde hair as she strolled along Aberystwyth's promenade. Despite the sunny day, her friend Eleri had seemed troubled when she'd called earlier, asking to meet at their favourite bench overlooking the bay.

Sure enough, when Mary approached the castle bench, she found Eleri sitting with her shoulders hunched, picking at her fingernails. Her usually bright green eyes were clouded with worry.

"Alright, cariad?" Mary asked as she sat down. You could see the whole harbour from the high vantage point of the castle ruins. Mr Pritchard was walking his dog down the main promenade.

Eleri moved her head from side to side, auburn hair falling across her face. "It's John. You saw how he was in the bakery."

Mary tensed, her full attention on Eleri. "I know. I thought he'd finally left you alone. I was shocked."

"So was I." Eleri shivered despite the warm breeze. "But now he's talking nonsense about some inheritance from Aunt Ffion."

"Inheritance?" Mary frowned. She'd never heard Eleri's late aunt mentioned in terms of money. "I never got to hear what he was saying."

Nodding, Eleri explained how John had confronted her about a valuable locket Ffion supposedly bequeathed to Eleri before she died last year.

How, according to John, the locket was worth a small fortune, which he felt entitled to since Eleri had callously abandoned him to pursue her dreams in Aberystwyth.

Mary listened in dismay as Eleri described John's unreasonable demands, his voice rising in anger when Eleri insisted she had no such locket.

"But Ffion didn't leave you anything like that, did she?" Mary asked.

"No!" Eleri cried. "She didn't even own a valuable locket when she died. John's clearly lost his mind. I have a locket, but I found it at the beach the day I scattered Ffion's ashes. He can't have a claim on that!"

Mary pursed her lips. She'd never fully trusted John, knowing his selfish tendencies, but her heart sank as she realised she'd thought he changed. That night at the pub, he'd seemed so funny and thoughtful. What went wrong? Eleri had been right to leave him, inheritance or not. Still, John's bizarre behaviour recently signalled he might be growing unstable.

Mary sighed and shook her head. "Don't worry, cariad. I'll sort this out."

Eleri pressed her palm with a shaky smile. "Thank you. I can't keep looking over my shoulder, wondering if he's going to turn up making more wild accusations. I can't ask Gareth, he's done enough."

"Leave it to me," Mary assured her. "Enjoy the sunshine. And don't forget Aunt Ffion's famous vanilla sponge recipe you promised you're trying today! I don't know what you are putting in your cakes, but I'm not putting any weight on. And that's just licence to eat more!" She winked.

With a determined stride, Mary set off for John's accounting firm across town. She wouldn't let Eleri's ex poison her friend's fresh start in Aberystwyth.

The office building loomed like a monument to John's ego. The best in town. Mary brushed her blonde hair from her eyes and smoothed her dress before entering the office building. Hips swaying, she approached the receptionist with a wide smile.

"Hello, I'm here to see John Davies."

The receptionist blinked. "Do you have an appointment?"

"No, but tell him it's Mary Jones. He'll want to see me." She smiled sweetly, hiding her rage. Staring pointedly at the phone.

The receptionist dialled a number and pointed down the hall.

"These are rented offices. Today, John Davies is down the hall, second right.

"Thank you." Mary gave her brightest smile. It wasn't her fault John was a prize nob.

She sauntered down the corridor and let herself in. Surprise flashed across John's handsome features. Though furious, Mary couldn't deny he was appealing. Damn him. His crisp suit accentuated his athletic build, but his charming smile didn't reach his icy blue eyes.

"Mary Jones. What a pleasant surprise," John said smoothly. Too smoothly. Mary noticed his eyes flick warily to the open office door.

"Oh, don't pretend you're happy to see me," Mary shot back, crossing her arms tightly across her chest.

John gestured to a chair, but Mary stayed on her feet, glaring at him defiantly. She thought she spotted a vein pulse in his temple. Good - she wanted him unsettled.

"We need to talk. In private," Mary added pointedly with a glance toward the door.

John's jaw pulsed briefly, but he moved to shut the office door with a quiet click. "Well?" he asked tersely, leaning back against the solid oak desk with studied nonchalance.

Mary inhaled deeply before unleashing her disappointment. "How could you treat Eleri like that, making bizarre accusations about some inheritance?" She despised the way her voice shook, betraying her rage.

John flinched at the accusation, then scowled, his broad shoulders taught. "I have every right to what's mine. She's kept something valuable from me." His voice was laced with indignation.

Mary fought to keep her voice steady. "Nothing is yours, John. Ffion didn't leave Eleri any locket or inheritance apart from the bakery."

John raked a hand through his hair, laughing derisively. "And you know this how, exactly?" His tone dripped condescension.

"Because I know Eleri, and I know you're spouting utter rubbish to justify harassing her."

John turned away, bracing his hands on his desk. His knuckles whitened. "Do you have any idea what I've lost?" He practically spat the words.

The pain in his voice caught Mary off guard. She wavered, then forged ahead. "I know you're chasing something that doesn't exist. Just stop already, before you ruin Eleri's life."

John lifted his head, his icy eyes stormy. "So you're calling me a delusional liar now?" He pushed off from the desk, advancing toward Mary. She fought the urge to step back.

"I'm saying these stupid accusations won't bring back your relationship with Eleri," she replied, lifting her chin. "Let go of the past before you destroy her future." Mary scoffed, "A locket? John, think about how irrational that sounds. This isn't like you."

"You don't know me," John retorted.

Stung, Mary shot back, "I know you're not the type to make idiot accusations over money. Eleri says this aunt didn't even own any locket. Are you calling her a liar?"

John shifted, avoiding Mary's gaze. "I'm not calling her a liar, but Gareth said—"

"Gareth?" Mary interrupted. "What does he have to do with this?"

John's face flushed. "I overheard him telling Eleri about some antique locket she'd inherited. Worth a fortune."

Mary shook her head firmly. "Eleri inherited no such thing. I think you misunderstood. What do you expect when you were eavesdropping?"

"My own girlfriend wouldn't lie to me!" John insisted, but uncertainty tinged his voice.

"She's not your girlfriend anymore," Mary said bluntly. "You have no claim to anything of hers."

John flinched at her words. Pacing the office, he ruffled his hair with his hand. "I just thought if she sold this locket, we could get back what we'd lost. Start fresh."

Understanding dawned on Mary. This hysteria came from heartbreak, not greed. Her anger softened.

"John, you have to move on," she said. "Chasing something that doesn't exist won't bring the past back. Only you can build a new future, but it has to be without Eleri."

John halted, the fight draining from his imposing frame. His shoulders slumped in defeat. "You're right," he finally admitted. "This is madness."

The tension dissipated. She had got through to him.

Mary's heart ached over her own crushed fantasies. But Eleri mattered more.

Softening her tone, she continued. "Look, Eleri made her choice, and dwelling on the past won't change that. Maybe it's time to think about what you want going forward. Because what you're doing now? It's going nowhere."

John turned his gaze to the window. Mary let the silence stretch, hoping her words were sinking in.

Finally, he let out a long breath. "I just want the life I planned back," he admitted quietly.

Mary nodded. She couldn't condone how he'd handled things, but she understood why he felt the way he did.

"The past is gone," she said. "Nothing will bring it back. But you can still build something worthwhile if you let go of old hurts. Focus that energy into improving your own life, not tearing Eleri's down."

John lifted his shoulders wearily. "Maybe you're right. It's not like harassing her on the street will change anything." He met Mary's eyes. "I will leave her alone."

Mary exhaled in relief. "Thank you. That's the right decision."

As she turned to leave, John called out, "How does she seem in herself? Happy?"

Mary paused, debating how much to say. Finally, she replied, "She's still healing. But being back home, doing what she loves... she's getting there."

John nodded, looking pensive. Mary hoped her words would stick, convincing him to turn the page on this painful chapter at last.

With a sad smile, she turned to leave, blonde hair bouncing. "Goodbye, John."

Stepping outside into the late afternoon sun, Mary smiled, already picturing the joy on Eleri's face when she heard John had backed off. With that storm cloud lifted, Eleri could embrace her new beginning.

****

Eleri hummed to herself as she dried the last mixing bowl, the sweet scent of baking vanilla sponge still lingering in the air. When Mary had stopped by earlier with the wonderful news about John, Eleri had felt lighter than she had in weeks.

She could finally relax, knowing her obsessive ex had agreed to move on at last. No more paranoid glances over her shoulder or lying awake wondering if he'd show up making more weird accusations. The dark cloud that had been shadowing her sunny new life in Aberystwyth had lifted.

Smiling, Eleri untied her flour-dusted apron and headed upstairs to the flat that felt like home again. She had a rare evening off and intended to celebrate this newfound freedom.

After a long bubble bath, Eleri changed into her favourite floaty purple dress, and let her auburn hair curl around her face. She kept her makeup light, enhancing her natural glow.

Checking herself in the mirror, she nodded in satisfaction. She felt as carefree as the girl who'd left Aberystwyth a decade ago, chasing love and opportunity. Back then, she hadn't realised that genuine happiness was here all along.

Her phone chimed with a new message. It was from Gareth, asking if she was still up for dinner tonight.

Eleri smiled and quickly typed back: Can't wait! Meet you at 7.

Grabbing a cropped jacket against the evening breeze, she slipped on low heels and headed out. The setting sun cast a golden sheen over the harbour as she walked toward the restaurant overlooking the glittering water.

She spotted Gareth waiting outside, hands tucked in his pockets. His rugged features softened into a smile when he saw her, his mop of unruly hair falling across his forehead.

"You look amazing," he said, a flicker of admiration in his warm brown eyes.

Eleri's cheeks flushed happily. "You scrub up nice yourself," she teased. He looked unfairly handsome in a fitted sweater that showed off his muscular frame.

Offering his arm, he escorted her inside the elegant seafood restaurant. Soft jazz music drifted through the candlelit room as they settled at an intimate table beside the window.

Over grilled sea bass and seared scallops, Eleri told him about Mary's conversation with John. "I'm just relieved I can stop worrying. He'll turn up making wacky claims. I mean, he did it twice!"

Gareth shook his head, his jaw tightening briefly. "Good thing Mary set him straight. Though if he'd shown his face again, I'd have had a word myself."

Eleri smiled, knowing Gareth meant it. He'd been endlessly supportive over the last few months as she'd rebuilt her life in Aberystwyth, helping her get the bakery up and running. She didn't know what she would've done without him.

And maybe, just maybe, the spark she increasingly felt between them could grow into something more. The wine and candlelight were making her feel bolder. She reached across the table to brush his fingers with her own.

"I'm glad you were here for me through everything," she said.

Gareth turned his hand towards hers, his thumb tracing slow circles over her knuckles. "Always," he murmured, holding her gaze.

Eleri's heart fluttered like a wild bird in her chest. She knew Gareth cared for her. But was he ready to leave the friend zone behind? Staring into his chocolate brown eyes, she thought she saw a reflection of her own longing.

The dessert menu lay forgotten as they talked and laughed, hands loosely entwined across the table. The dining room seemed to melt away until it was just the two of them cocooned in this perfect moment.

Gareth walked Eleri home after dinner, matching his long strides to her meandering pace. Neither was eager for this perfect evening to end. The sea front was bare, with only a few dog walkers to share the night.

As they ambled along the harbour promenade, the full moon shimmered across the water. Eleri stole glances at Gareth's profile, his slightly crooked nose and strong jaw cast in an alluring silhouette. Was he also avoiding her gaze, suddenly shy?

"Remember that red kite festival here years ago?" Gareth asked, breaking the silence.

Eleri smiled wistfully. "Of course! We were only teenagers, but I thought it was so romantic. I can't believe I was only fifteen!"

She recalled watching the kites swoop and circle with Gareth, acutely aware of how close their bodies were on the packed hillside. The same tingling hyperawareness she felt now.

"I almost kissed you that day," Gareth admitted with a small grin, his eyes fixed on the horizon. "Chickened out at the last minute."

Eleri's pulse quickened. She leaned on the promenade railing, gazing out at the glittering bay to still her hope.

Gareth joined her, his elbow just barely grazing hers. The subtle contact sent shivers rippling through her whole body.

"Part of me wishes you had kissed me. I would have known you liked me," Eleri said, daring to reveal her long-buried feelings.

Gareth turned toward her, his face showing mingled longing and uncertainty. Their lips hovered a hairsbreadth apart.

"I wish I had too," he whispered.

Eleri swayed instinctively closer, drawn into his orbit... but Gareth caught her shoulders, stilling her.

"Not yet," he murmured. With aching slowness, he brushed his nose against hers, teasing her with possibilities.

They walked the rest of the way in tantalising anticipation, the romantic tension building. Outside the bakery, the sea air felt charged with possibility. Eleri turned to him. "Thank you for a wonderful evening," she said, suddenly shy.

Gareth tucked a strand of hair behind her ear, his fingers trailing along her jaw. "It doesn't have to end yet," he said, his voice low.

Heart racing, Eleri looked up at him. Slowly, he leaned down and brushed his lips against hers.

The kiss was soft, tentative - a question. Eleri answered by wrapping her arms around his neck and pulling him closer.

When their lips finally met, the kiss was a blaze of pent-up passion, made even sweeter by the exquisite wait.

Chapter 13

The ruined walls of the ancient castle stood bathed in moonlight, the pale stones bearing centuries of history in their cracked and eroded facades. Gareth traced his fingers along the weathered crenels and merlons, feeling the stories buried within these ancient stone ramparts. Below them, waves lapped rhythmically against the stone wall. There was no one around. Just like he planned.

Beside him, Eleri gazed up at a crumbling archway, eyes following the shape now worn with age. Short, cut-grass surrounded the man-made structures. He had never seen anyone cut the grass, but it never seemed to grow. He could imagine the rulers of old walking these same ramparts, peering out over domain and sea just as he and Eleri did now. In the moon's glow, the ruins seemed alive with whispers of the past.

Gareth's mind drifted back to when they were teenagers, full of fanciful imagination. "Remember when we used to pretend we ruled this castle?" he asked Eleri with a grin.

Eleri's eyes lit up at the memory. "Oh yes! I was the warrior queen Branwen, defending the castle from invaders." She mimed wielding a sword, her fiery hair blowing in the breeze.

"While I was the brave knight who won your heart after many feats of courage," Gareth said. He struck a dashing pose.

Eleri laughed. "We spun such epic tales back then. Battles and betrayals, allies and enemies, affairs of the heart." She gazed thoughtfully at a crumbling tower. "We must have walked every inch of these ruins acting out scenes."

"We were so dramatic! John and I duelling with sticks for your honour and all that." Gareth picked up a broken tree branch, brandishing it theatrically.

Eleri's eyes sparkled with nostalgia. "I miss those days sometimes. To be young and daft again."

Gareth lowered the branch, his playful smile fading. "Me too, cariad. Me too."

"It's so peaceful here," Eleri murmured. She closed her eyes, drawing in a long breath as if to capture the salt air inside her. When she opened them again, her gaze fixed on Gareth, vivid even in the darkness. "I'd forgotten how lovely the castle can be at night."

Gareth nodded, throat tightening. With Eleri here, the ruins held a magic he recalled from their teenage years - a sense of history and possibility.

Gareth glanced over at Eleri, her auburn hair shining in the soft light, a tentative smile playing on her lips. He still couldn't believe he'd convinced her to join him on this impromptu midnight picnic, pilfering cakes and sandwiches from her own bakery that afternoon.

"What a sneaky trick," Eleri had chided, eyes glinting with amusement as she unboxed the treats from her bakery. "Luring me here with my own wares."

"I never claimed to fight fair, cariad," Gareth grinned.

Now they sat amongst crumbling walls destroyed by a war long ago, the sounds of the sea a soothing backdrop to the stillness. He watched Eleri, startled by the green even in the darkness, lit only by a fat candle encased in glass.

"Remember that solstice party in year twelve?" Eleri laughed, the sound warming him more than the tea. "God, we were absolutely trollied. I'm amazed we didn't fall off the parapet."

"Hey now, I was completely sober," Gareth protested. At her sceptical look, he amended, "Mostly sober."

They grinned at each other, the intervening years since school falling away. He could still envision a young Eleri, eyes shining with laughter and mischief as she pulled him by the hand up the winding staircase, shushing his drunken giggles as the dawn had emerged gentle and rosy, infusing the grey stones in molten gold.

"That was the summer everything changed," Eleri murmured, almost to herself, smile fading. "You helped your da... I went off to university with John. We stopped coming here."

Gareth busied himself tidying their picnic remains, jaw clenched at the mention of that pillock's name. He knew she'd broken it off with John months ago, finally seeing his true selfish colours. But the prat's shadow still lingered between them like a bothersome ghost.

Eleri seemed to read his thoughts, laying a hand on his arm. "Hey. John's gone, he's given up. I'm here now. With you." Her green eyes reflected the moonlight earnestly.

Gareth softened, turning his hand to intertwine their fingers. "I know, cariad, just..." He broke off, frustrated. "I hate how he took advantage of you. You deserve so much better."

Like me, he wanted to add, but the words stuck maddeningly in his throat. You coward.

Eleri gave him a sad smile. "The heart wants what it wants, even when it shouldn't. But enough brooding - we're not those lovesick kids anymore." She bumped his shoulder playfully, the contact zinging through him. He was hyperaware of her nearness, the floral scent of her shampoo mingling with the sea air.

Gareth's throat tightened as they stood together amidst the moonlit husk of the former fortress. The ruins fell into silence, only the distant lap of waves filling the night. Gareth's pulse quickened as he and Eleri locked eyes in the moonlight. She gave him a tentative smile, hands clasped together in unconscious expectation. He drew a shaky breath, acutely aware of her nearness.

The ancient stones surrounding them seemed charged with purpose, waiting for something momentous to occur. Eleri's eyes shone brighter than the waning moon, fixed intently on him. Gareth swayed closer, caught in her gravitational pull. His hand lifted of its own volition to brush a windblown strand of hair from her cheek.

Eleri's lips parted at his touch, her quickened breathing matching his own. The ruins held their breath with them, time suspended, balanced on the cusp of a fateful, life-altering instant...

Gareth's pulse quickened with her proximity. Now was the time for confessions, he knew, but the words stuck in his throat. So instead, he drew Eleri wordlessly into his arms, leaning in for a kiss, just as a furry, energetic bullet of a puppy came bounding through the ruins towards them.

"Moron! Where's that blasted beast gone and run off to now?" Mr Pritchard's annoyed shout echoed from nearby.

The exuberant Border Collie puppy made a beeline for Eleri and Gareth, his tags jingling and paws scrabbling eagerly on the stones. Before they could react, Moron leapt up and planted two large, muddy paws squarely on Eleri's jacket, licking her face excitedly.

"Ych a fi, down boy!" Eleri laughed despite herself, ruffling the pup's wiry fur as she gently pushed him off. Moron paid her no mind, already squeezing himself between them to nose enthusiastically at their picnic basket, his stubby tail wagging madly.

"Moron!"

"Sorry, Mr Pritchard?" Eleri blinked.

"Moron, the blasted puppy." Mr Pritchard laughed at her expression. "Have you forgotten all your Welsh while you were away?"

"Oh," she turned as red as Mr Pritchard, "You named your puppy after his colouring. Or does he like carrots?"

"Both cariad," the older man was obviously fighting exasperation and mirth as he watched Moron move towards the basket.

"Shame on you, you little demon!" Gareth scolded through his laughter as Moron thrust his head fully into the basket and rummaged for goodies. He could only watch helplessly as sandwiches tumbled out onto the grass, cookie crumbs and crisp shards scattering everywhere. Moron gave them a devilish look, dribbling chilli relish and practically grinning through a mouthful of stolen roast beef.

"Moron! Get back here, you mangy mutt!" Mr Pritchard's

voice echoed from the castle walls as he huffed, trying to get his breath, wheezing like a chimney. "Wretched pup's going to be the death of me. And stop stealing people's suppers, you mutt!"

Moron merely wagged his tail faster at the attention, sending their empty flask rolling down the stone steps with a wet nose nudge.

"We tried to catch him, Mr Pritchard, but he was too quick," Gareth said.

"That scoundrel's half rabbit, I tell you," Mr Pritchard grumbled, bracing his hands on his knees to catch his breath.

Eleri bit her lip, stifling a grin at the older man whose face matched his pup's russet fur.

"At least he didn't gobble down the entire basket," she said kindly, scooping up the dropped sandwiches and brushing off the dirt and crumbs. "Though he may regret the chilli relish later."

Moron seemed to take that as a challenge, gulping down another sandwich and licking his chops before scampering towards the ruins again.

"Oi, get back here!" Gareth shouted, lunging after the escaped pup. Moron yipped playfully, staying just out of reach as he led Gareth on a merry chase through the maze of moonlit archways and tumbled walls. He skittered over the grass, sending Gareth diving after him in vain while Eleri and Mr Pritchard watched in amusement.

"You've met your match, boyo," called Mr Pritchard. "He's quick as a whip, that one.

Moron scurried figure eights around Gareth's legs, nipping teasingly at his trouser cuffs and scooting away whenever Gareth got close to grabbing his collar. The pup's fur was coarse under his fingers whenever he managed a brief ruffle before Moron squirmed gleefully away again.

Gareth panted, wiping his brow as Moron trotted just out of reach, tail held jauntily high. "You win this round, you little monster," he conceded. Moron barked happily and bounded back to nose Gareth's empty hands.

"None left, mate. You cleared us out," Gareth chuckled, giving the pup a conciliatory scratch behind the ears. Moron licked his fingers, then scampered back to Eleri for more ill-gotten treats.

"Menace," she scolded affectionately, handing Moron a final leftover crust which he gobbled down immediately. "I hope we've worn you out a bit, for Mr Pritchard's sake."

"Doubtful, but I appreciate you trying," Mr Pritchard sighed. "Best get this blighter home before he destroys what's left of the castle." He clipped a lead onto Moron's collar, who immediately strained against it, eager for his next adventure.

"Sorry again, Mr Pritchard. He's certainly a spirited one," Gareth said.

"Too right. Nothing but trouble and mess," Mr Pritchard grumbled. But he patted Moron's head fondly. "Don't know how we manage without him. Gets me up and moving, even if it's chasing the blasted beast from one end of the town to the other."

Gareth and Eleri chuckled. "Take care," Eleri called as Moron led Mr Pritchard back down the winding stairs.

She turned to Gareth with a smile. "Never a dull moment here, is there?"

He laughed. "Certainly not with a madcap like Moron causing chaos."

Their merriment faded as they gazed at each other, a sudden tension descending once more. The ruins were silent save for the distant waves, enshrouded in haunting beauty beneath the moon's glow.

"Why would you call your dog Moron? I know it means carrot, even so," Whispered Eleri.

"I think he was annoyed his wife got a puppy at first," whispered Gareth back in case the old man could still hear him. Louder, "We may as well go home after that excitement."

"I'm sorry Gareth, it was lovely." She picked up the mugs and stooped to pick up the flask from where the dog had nosed it down some steps and began putting them in the old woven basket.

A fierce wind gusted through the ruins, making them stumble apart. Gareth stared around wildly as debris from their picnic swirled dangerously through the air.

"What the hell?" Eleri gasped, grabbing his hand.

Gareth and Eleri leaned into the wind as it whipped Eleri's hair across her face. She turned her back to shield her eyes. Gareth grabbed her arm to steady them both against the buffeting gusts. Dust and debris swirled up from the ground, pelting their legs. Eleri cried out as the wind nearly lifted her off her feet.

As fast as it came, the wind dissipated. Gareth and Eleri steadied themselves, ears ringing in the sudden quiet. Eleri's hair settled softly back into place. They exchanged astonished looks in the heavy silence left behind.

Gareth tightened his grip on Eleri's trembling hand, the pulse thundering. "Are you alright, cariad?"

She nodded, shaking. "What was that? It felt... angry. Like we did something wrong."

A prickle of unease crept down Gareth's spine at her words. He glanced around warily at the now-peaceful ruins, bathed in moonlight once more. They heard barking in the distance, and the occasional "Moron!" in an exasperated voice.

"Just a freak gust off the sea," he said, trying to sound convincing. But the wind had seemed too focused, too malicious. As if intent on reprimanding them.

A flicker of movement caught his eye, and he turned with a jolt. For the briefest moment, he thought he saw a pale, ghostly figure hovering near a crumbling archway, watching them. Blinking rapidly, he saw only empty night.

"Did you see that?" he whispered.

Eleri followed his gaze, brows drawn together. "See what?"

Gareth hesitated. It had to be his imagination, surely. "Nothing. Just a trick of the light."

He glanced down to see Eleri shivering and cursed himself for letting the strange occurrence rattle him. She needed warming up, not more crazy tales of ghosts.

"Here." Gareth wrapped his jacket around her shoulders,

rubbing her arms briskly. "Let's get you back before you freeze."

Eleri nodded, huddling into his jacket. As they turned toward the winding stairs, Gareth cast one last look over his shoulder at the silent ruins. For a heartbeat, he thought he saw the pale figure again, fading in and out of the shadows.

You're stalling, coward, it seemed to whisper. Tell her how you feel.

Gareth blinked hard, breath catching. Then the apparition vanished, leaving only moonlit stones once more.

You're losing your bloody mind, he told himself. But the uneasy prickle remained as they descended the stairs. A question lodged in his heart.

What if the ghostly whispers spoke the truth?

Chapter 14

The musty scent of ancient pages mingled with the smell of baking bread in the cramped basement below Eleri's bakery. She coughed, waving away cobwebs as she followed Gareth down the creaky wooden steps.

"What did you want to show me again?" Eleri asked, rubbing her arms briskly as she shivered in the dank chill.

Gareth glanced back, his dark eyes glinting in the dim light. "I found something earlier, buried behind those old crates, when I was storing some antiques." He stooped to meet her eyes, his breath warm on her face. "I don't think I've actually said thank you properly for letting me store and sell my antiques here while my shop is being refurbished. I'm sorry it's taking so long."

Eleri smiled, thinking of the ambience the eclectic pieces brought to her cafe. "It's not all altruism, Gareth. I do get revolving decor out of it. People are actually coming in to see what's changed each week."

His deep chuckle echoed off the brick walls. He pointed to a shadowy alcove along the far wall. "Look."

Frowning, Eleri squirmed past stacks of supplies and antique furniture, avoiding cobwebs, brushing against her favourite green top, until she reached the alcove. The sight of a weathered leather tome tucked away on a shelf greeted her. Strange symbols shimmered in the wan light motes filtering down from the stairs and through the high window. She reached out, hesitating. This must be a clue. Why else would Gareth drag her down here? Her trembling fingers brushed off the dust, revealing intricate Celtic designs someone had painted in gold and silver on the cover that seemed to twist before her eyes.

Eleri swallowed hard. "What is this?" she whispered.

Gareth came up behind her, his solid warmth comforting against the basement's chill. "I think it's connected to the curse."

Eleri's heart skipped a beat before resuming its pounding rhythm. Ever since Gareth stumbled upon the cryptic book in his shop, she couldn't sleep because of the worry of the ancient curse on the women in her family line. Doomed romances, lives cut short, history repeating in an endless melancholic cycle. Her mother had been alone, and she'd never seen Ffion with anyone... She shivered, drawing her cardigan tighter against an imagined icy breeze.

Taking a breath, Eleri opened the tome's brittle pages. Faded ink swam before her eyes in the dim light, indecipherable beside aged photos. She turned the pages with trembling fingers, scanning for any legible words.

"It looks like a scrapbook! But most of it is in Welsh." Eleri squinted at the text. "I can make out a name... Carys Evans. And a date - January 1893."

Gareth moved closer, also scanning the pages. "Yes, this book is over a century old. Look how damaged the pages are. Water has made a lot of the ink run and fade." He gingerly turned a few more pages. "There's another date - 1909. And here..."

Gareth's voice trailed off as his eyes locked onto the photograph tucked into the dusty old book. Eleri followed his intent stare, her breath catching as she saw the two strangers wearing those familiar antique lockets. This was what they were looking for.

The gloom of the basement made it hard to see the image despite the light from the small window.

"Why don't we take this upstairs where there's better light?" Eleri suggested, shivering against the chill.

Gareth looked sheepish, realising he could have just brought the book up to begin with. "Sorry, I just got so excited down here I wasn't thinking straight." He mumbled.

"Let's get out of this cold basement." Eleri closed the book and headed for the stairs, Gareth following behind at her heels.

They hurried up to the sitting room, welcoming the warmth seeping from the kitchen on the ground floor. It was at times like this that she appreciated living above a bakery. The afternoon trade hadn't started yet, and Mary was looking after the café in exchange for sponge cake. Eleri sat down in the window seat next to the window. Gareth joined her.

"That's much better." Eleri declared, angling the book to catch the afternoon sunlight. The gilt edging on the pages glittered as she turned them to find where they had left off in the dim basement. Now they could examine the photograph better.

"They're wearing the lockets! This is huge," Eleri exclaimed. She turned through the pages. "If we can find out who they were, maybe it will lead us to the other one."

Most of the surrounding pages were too damaged to read. Eleri flipped back to the photo, hands shaking. "Can you make out anything on this page?"

Gareth leaned in, eyes narrowed in concentration as he tried to decipher the faded handwriting. "It's difficult... looks like poetry or song lyrics perhaps..." He traced a finger along the ancient script, mumbling possible translations under his breath.

Eleri watched his profile, noting the strength in his stubbled jaw, the intensity in his deep brown eyes. She still couldn't quite believe someone like him was here with her, drawn together by both fate and choice. She tamped down the rising fear that it was only temporary, that the curse would tear them apart as it had done for generations before. Eleri fidgeted beside him, nerves coiled tight. She willed him to find some clue, some key to unlocking the curse's sinister mystery. Seconds stretched into minutes as Gareth puzzled over the text.

He exhaled sharply. "I think I've got something. A phrase here, difficult to make out, but I think it mentions the women of your family, the tragic lovers..."

Eleri's breath became shallower, palms sweating. "And the curse?"

Gareth scanned ahead, translating with a halting voice. "Darkness born of spite and envy, time-twisted yet ever renewed. Two souls united, fate divided, only... only when the past is paid shall joy prevail..."

He trailed off, meeting her frightened eyes. Eleri's stomach twisted itself into knots, bile rising in her throat as the dire revelations sank in. She traced a finger over the aged parchment, shuddering as its ominous words seemed to confirm her worst fears. The curse was real. Tangible. Written into history through ink and leather binding.

A slow, icy chill slithered down Eleri's spine, dread pooling in her core even as she desperately tried to deny the evidence before her eyes. She wanted to believe it was fiction, but this was irrefutable proof now, sat before her in an old scrapbook. The cryptic phrasing echoed what they already knew, but somehow, seeing it written in ink made the curse real.

"We're going to lose each other," she choked out, tears spilling down her cheeks. "Every lifetime, over and over... My family never finding love that lasts..."

She trailed off, looking at Gareth, his focus on the book. Did she love him? She had feelings for him; she knew that. Eleri examined her feelings tentatively. God, she did! But the question was, did he? He hadn't said it. They'd only been together awhile. It was too soon. She'd spent years with John and never felt real love. Maybe Gareth felt the same way about her as she did about John. What if this curse doomed her to a life without love by choosing the wrong men?

Eleri's vision blurred as helpless sobs wracked her body. The weight of generations crushed down upon her, an inevitability she was powerless to change. She tried to speak, to voice the dread curdling within, but her throat clenched tight, allowing only ragged gasps to escape. Her chest heaved as she struggled to draw breath, pulse thundering in her ears. She pressed a hand over her heart as if to hold in the sick fear threatening to overwhelm her.

Gareth enveloped her in his strong arms, the solid warmth of him cleaving through the storm of her emotions. As she clung to him, tears dampening his shirt, Eleri focused on slowing her ragged breaths. In and out, until the vise around her throat loosened. The weight of inevitability threatened to separate her and Gareth before they'd barely had a chance to be together.

She squeezed her eyes shut, willing away helpless tears. His muscular arms embraced her, then smoothed back her hair, pressing a kiss to her temple.

"We're not going to let some centuries-old curse dictate our future," he murmured. "Damn fate. I'm not losing you, Eleri, no matter what some mouldy old book says."

A weak laugh escaped her lips even as she clung tighter, afraid to let go. "But how can we stop something like this? It feels so much bigger than us."

Gareth cupped her face, brushing away the wetness on her cheek with his thumb. "We'll find a way," he promised, conviction burning in his eyes. "This curse was born out of bitterness and jealousy, right? So... we defeat it through light and love. Having hope, staying faithful. Not taking a single moment together for granted."

Eleri searched his eyes, trying to draw strength from the determination she found there. The sincerity and depth of his feelings shone through, easing her fears for the moment. She managed a tremulous smile.

"You think we can break the cycle?"

"I know we can," Gareth stated without hesitation. "Whatever it takes, however long, I'll never stop fighting for us. We write our own destinies now. We know where one locket is - we just need to find out who this man is in the photo. It will give us a clue." He covered her hands with his, meeting her concerned look. "There is hope, cariad."

Eleri pulled him down into a fierce kiss, pouring all her love and trust into it. Gareth responded, the familiar heat of his mouth and hands igniting her senses until she felt drunk, anchored only by his strong form. For these stolen moments at least, hope and passion drowned out the curse's dark whispers.

They finally broke apart, breaths ragged. Gareth rested his

forehead against hers. The corner of his mouth quirked in a playful smirk that made Eleri's knees weak.

"This curse has nothing on us, cariad," he murmured. "We're too stubborn and wilful to surrender without a fight. The past can't dictate the future - we make our own fate."

Eleri smiled fully now, buoyed by his confidence. "Too right we do," she agreed, heart lifting. She placed a quick kiss on his lips before stepping back. "Come on then. We've got a bakery slash cafe slash antique shop to open."

Gareth took her hand, giving it a pat. As they turned to leave, Eleri cast one last conflicted glance at the book. The dire words within evoked a chill premonition, but she refused to let it douse her spark of hope. For now, she tucked away the book's unsettling revelations and focused on making each moment count.

She reached up to grasp the silver locket hanging around her neck, tracing her fingers over the intricate Celtic knot design. The metal seemed to give off a faint hum with an energy she couldn't explain.

Eleri closed her eyes, saying a silent prayer that they could somehow find the matching locket, that they could break the sinister cycle that had torn apart so many of her family before them.

When they reached the bottom of the stairs, Eleri blinked hard to adjust her eyes to the bakery's bright lighting. The basement's shadowy chill clung to her, making the cheerful sunlit warmth seem almost surreal.

Mary was sitting by the counter, tucking into her cake, looking guilty. Eleri laughed.

"Why are you looking like you've just stolen the crown jewels, cariad? I said you could have whatever you wanted for helping me out."

"Um, it's my second piece." Her face went a deeper red.

Eleri drew her into a hug. "It's not like the cakes are affecting your weight. You look amazing, And I really appreciate your help. Fancy a cuppa?"

At her friend's nod, she busied herself heating water for tea, her friend's chatter and the ritual grounded her rattled nerves.

As she waited for the kettle to boil, Eleri glanced out the window into the street. Everything appeared normal, yet she couldn't shake the feeling of mysterious energies enveloping her and Gareth like currents in a shadowy stream.

The fine hairs on Eleri's nape prickled as though tendrils of icy vapour teased along her skin. She rubbed her arms, trying to shake the creeping sensation of phantom breaths gusting against her.

Eleri shot a glance at Mary, but she gave no sign anything was wrong. She bit her lip, fighting the urge to peer over her shoulder into the empty corners swathed in shadow. The forces swirling around them remained unseen, intangible apart from their chilling caress, raising gooseflesh along her arms.

The screech of the kettle made her jump. Heart pounding, Eleri's hands trembled as she poured the tea, nearly scalding herself. She forced her breathing to slow, willing her heart to stop racing.

A creak on the stairs had her whipping around, pulse skittering. But it was only Gareth coming up from the basement, his expression solemn.

"I was going to hide the book away again, but..." He hesitated, glancing back toward the basement door. "I don't like leaving it down there unattended. It feels... hungry, almost. Like it wants to be read."

Eleri suppressed a shudder, gaze darting nervously around the bakery. She couldn't shake the growing sense of unseen forces swirling around them, primed to descend at any moment.

"What if we can't stop it?" she whispered. "The curse. What if it takes you from me no matter what we do?"

Gareth crossed the room in quick strides, pulling her into his arms. "That won't happen," he insisted firmly. But she could hear the slightest waver in his voice.

Eleri clung to him, a profound dread chilling her bones despite the sunshine's warmth.

Chapter 15

"Rise and shine, cariad!" Gareth's cheerful voice stirred Eleri from sleep. Sunlight streamed through her bedroom window as he entered with a breakfast tray.

"What's all this?" Eleri asked, sitting up in bed.

"Just wanted to surprise my best girl." Gareth kissed her forehead and set the tray across her lap. "I was thinking we could take a little holiday. Get out of Aber for a bit. What do you say?"

Eleri smiled, taking a sip of coffee. A weekend away with Gareth sounded perfect. "I'd love that. Did you have anywhere in mind?"

"Well, I wanted to take you to Paris, but there aren't any flights, trains, or ferries there today, strikes apparently, so I thought about this charming inn near Cardiff that we could check out. We could explore the city; try that new Italian place you've been wanting to visit. I already booked us a room for tonight."

"You're the best!" Eleri threw her arms around him, nearly upsetting the tray. A weekend of romance and freedom was exactly what she needed.

After breakfast, while Gareth went to get his car, Eleri rushed downstairs to the bakery. She felt a chill despite the sunny weather. She shook it off as excitement for the trip. But when she went to flip the "Open" sign to "Closed," the sign wouldn't budge. After several hard tugs, it flipped easily, as if some invisible force had been holding it in place.

Strange, Eleri thought. She'd never had trouble with the sign before. A prickle on the back of her neck made her turn around, but she saw nothing wrong in the empty bakery. With a shrug, she continued her closing duties, the odd incident slipping from her mind.

As Eleri locked the bakery door, a croaky voice spoke behind her. "Going somewhere, dearie?"

She turned to see old Mrs Harris, who lived above the bookshop next door. Her wispy white hair was pulled back in a messy bun, and her hunched frame was draped in a faded shawl. Her wrinkled face and milky blue eyes gave the impression of someone who had seen many years. The elderly woman was smiling, but her gaze unsettled Eleri.

"Just a little holiday out of town with Gareth," Eleri replied politely.

Mrs Harris clicked her tongue. "Oh, I wouldn't advise leaving Aberystwyth this weekend. Cardiff is a nightmare; some rugby match I hear. The stars are not aligned for travel right now."

A chill went through Eleri. How could Mrs Harris possibly know their travel plans? The old woman patted Eleri's shoulder with a bony hand.

"Trust me, dear. Stay close to home for now. The spirits tell me it's for the best." She ambled away, her cane clicking on the pavement before Eleri could respond.

The blood drained from Eleri's face, her heart racing with foreboding. The woman's warning echoed in her mind as she walked to meet Gareth. She tried to brush it off as the ramblings of an eccentric old lady, but doubt nagged at her. She started noticing details she had never paid much attention to before. The iron lampposts were adorned with intricate swirling graffiti resembling Celtic knots or magical runes. Strange symbols marked some of the old buildings' archways and windows. The seagulls circling the harbour had an eerie glow about their eyes.

Everything felt imbued with a subtle wrongness, as if the eccentric vibe of this seaside town hid something more sinister. Though Eleri had lived her whole life in Aberystwyth, apart from ten years, she reminded herself; she viewed it with new eyes, attuned to an aura of mystery and foreboding.

"Ready, cariad?" Gareth's voice at her shoulder made her jump. She blinked away the disorienting impressions and took his arm with a nod. Surely it was just nerves about their trip causing this ominous mood. Still, she shivered as they walked on, unable to shake the feeling of unseen eyes tracking their progress through Aberystwyth's narrow lanes.

"Absolutely!" Eleri slid into Gareth's car, giddy with excitement. She rolled down the window, letting the brisk sea air wash over her as they drove.

Aberystwyth was fading into the distance as they approached the A44. Suddenly, the car began sputtering.

"Not again," Gareth muttered, guiding it to the shoulder as the engine cut out entirely. He popped the bonnet, smoke rising into the air.

Eleri joined him. "Any chance of an easy fix?"

Gareth's frown provided the answer. With no other cars in sight, they weighed their options. The A44 stretched endlessly in both directions.

"Guess we're walking back in to town," Gareth said, taking Eleri's hand. After thirty minutes they reached Aberystwyth's outskirts, the car a tiny speck behind them. Eleri sighed. So much for their city getaway.

"This old car has been nothing but trouble lately," Gareth said as they trudged along. "Tell you what - I'll call a taxi to take us to the train station. We can still make that inn by evening if we hurry."

Eleri smiled up at him. "I knew I could count on you to solve this."

Gareth made the call, but they were all booked up.

"C'mon Eleri, it's not that far away. We can still catch it if we walk fast. The next train is in 45 minutes."

An hour later, they got back to outside Eleri's flat. She popped upstairs to get her campervan's keys, while Gareth went to get a snack. Only to find all four tires were flat when she got back down to the street.

"How on Earth?"

Gareth rounded the corner with two bacon butties in hand.

"What's wrong? Oh." He looked nonplussed for a moment

before handing her a butty. The aroma of bacon was irresistible, and her eyes nearly rolled back into her head.

"That good huh?" He said.

"You betcha. What are we going to do now?" She said, taking a bite.

"Plan B, or C, or whatever it is." He pulled up his phone and pulled up the train app. "Great, there's a train in 15 minutes for the 2 o'clock train. We can make it." He pressed the button to book it and grinned at her.

"You ready?" She nodded, and they raced down the street until they got to the main shops and veered down the road to the station.

"C'mon, I can see it." She called behind her.

He puffed, pulling her suitcase and his rucksack with the remnants of his bacon roll in his other hand.

They got there with 2 minutes to spare, giggling like teenagers to hear an announcement over the tannoy.

"We regret to inform all passengers that the 2 o'clock train to Cardiff has been delayed due to mechanical failure. We will update you with more information as we have it."

Groans echoed through the station. Gareth dragged a hand down his face.

"Of all the rotten luck..."

Eleri gave his arm a sympathetic pat. "It's okay, a delay isn't the end of the world. We can still make it work."

As it turned out, the train wouldn't be fixed for hours. The next one didn't depart until morning.

Gareth collapsed onto a bench, thoroughly disheartened. "I'm so sorry, Eleri. I hoped this weekend would be special for us."

"Oh, Gareth." She laced her fingers through his. "It's not your fault. These things happen."

His eyes softened as he smiled at her. "Have I told you lately that you're amazing?"

Eleri playfully bumped her shoulder against his. "Remember, I still have you here with me. That's all I need to make any day special."

By now, the winter sun was sinking below the horizon. As they exited the station, Gareth stopped.

"One more idea. It's a long shot, but..." He pulled out his phone, dialling swiftly, from the number on a poster in the wall. "Yes, I need a taxi to drive two passengers from Aberystwyth to Cardiff, leaving immediately... You can? Excellent!"

He relayed the pickup location, then ended the call, beaming at Eleri. "We've still got a chance!"

But when the taxi arrived twenty minutes later, doubt crossed the driver's face. "All the way to Cardiff, you say. Are you sure about that, mate?"

Gareth's shoulders slumped. "Is there a problem?"

The driver scratched his head. "It's just... I've never actually left Aber before. Always been plenty of business right here in town."

Gareth's eyes narrowed in suspicion. "That's not possible. How could you operate a taxi all these years and stay only in town?"

The driver shrugged. "Beats me! But I'm willing to give it a go if you are. Get in."

Eleri's tone grew soft. "It's odd, but let's see if he can get us there."

Gareth rubbed his eyes and shook his head, but he nodded and helped load their bags.

They piled into the taxi, exchanging quick glances and fidgeting with the straps of their bags. Anticipation hung in the air like an electric charge, crackling with every rustle of fabric and nervous laugh. The driver, sensing their enthusiasm, twisted in his seat to ask, his curiosity mirrored in the raised arch of his eyebrow and the tilt of his head.

"What's the address where you're going, mate?"

Gareth gave him the postcode and the driver put it into the sat nav.

The tick of the indicators let them know they were on their way.

"Continue on Terrace Road." The robotic voice blared, making Eleri jump.

"A bit loud." She muttered.

Seconds later, "After ten metres, turn right onto Thespian Road."

Gareth settled back in his seat, smiling at Eleri.

"See cariad, we're on our way."

"Turn right onto Alexander Road."

"I'm not sure about that, Gareth." Eleri pointed out the window. "That's the train station!"

"Continue on Terrace Road." The sat nav repeated as they passed the station.

"That's funny... I must have missed a turn." The driver murmured. "Ah well, we'll just take the next one."

Only there was no other turn. Round and round they wait. After a few more failed attempts to leave Aberystwyth, the driver let them out at the train station, thoroughly baffled.

"I'm stumped! In twenty years driving these streets, I've never encountered anything like this." He wished them luck and drove off into the night.

Gareth exploded. "This is absurd! It's like something out of the Twilight Zone." He whirled to Eleri. "How are you not more upset by this?"

"Getting angry won't help," Eleri said. "I'm sure there's a reasonable explanation." But doubt was creeping into her mind.

Gareth dragged a hand through his hair. "You think this is normal? What if... what if something is preventing us from leaving?"

Eleri shook her head with a reassuring smile. "You're letting frustration get the better of you. Try to stay positive."

But privately, she wondered if Gareth was right to be suspicious. This trip was cursed with an increasingly bizarre streak of bad luck. She shivered, the evening suddenly feeling colder.

Gareth stayed silent, brow furrowed, lips pressed together,

as they walked back to the flat. Eleri looped her arm through his, but his unease lingered. She wished she could smooth away the creases of concern from his face.

"We'll figure this out," she promised, leaning her head on his shoulder. Gareth's expression eased as he wrapped his arm around her waist, the frightful mysteries of the day seeming less ominous, with Eleri at his side.

Bank at the flat, Eleri hesitated before putting the key in her lock. What if Mrs Harris had been right? Gareth noticed her fear.

"What's wrong?"

Eleri shivered. "Just something my neighbour said. About not leaving Aberystwyth this weekend."

Gareth's eyes widened. "That's absurd. Just a coincidence, I'm sure." But he too glanced at next door warily as they entered the bakery.

Once inside, Eleri once again entwined her arm through Gareth's.

"I'm sorry our trip keeps getting derailed," he said, frustration in his voice. "I wanted this weekend to be perfect for us."

Eleri stopped and turned to face him. "Gareth, any time I get to spend with you is perfect, trip or no trip."

She cradled his face in her hands. "You're all I need. Just having you here, being together, that's what matters."

Gareth's jaw relaxed as he gazed at her. He pulled her close, brushing a loose strand of hair from her face. "How did I get so lucky to find you?"

Eleri's heart raced, being wrapped in his embrace. She tilted her chin up as his lips met hers in a deep, lingering kiss. The failed romantic getaway was forgotten as they lost themselves in each other.

Later, lying on the sofa looking out at the moonlit sea, Gareth played with her hair. "Maybe being stuck here isn't so bad after all."

Eleri smiled up at him. "As long as we're together, I'm exactly where I want to be."

Chapter 16

Eleri's rose from restless dreams. Her red hair spilling across her pillow like a nest of snakes. She slipped out of bed, thoughts drifting back to the strange events of yesterday. What could be preventing them from leaving Aberystwyth?

Eleri was startled by a knock at the door. As she opened it, she dashed her fingers through her hair, the enticing aroma of fresh coffee enveloped her. Gareth stood there, holding out a paper bag and two steaming cups, a smile spreading across Eleri's face at the welcoming sight. The rich scent beckoned her forward like a magical spell.

"Thought you could use a pick-me-up after everything that happened," Gareth said, his familiar crooked grin making Eleri's heart flutter.

Eleri smiled gratefully, the rich aroma already reviving her spirits. They settled onto the sofa, munching pastries as the coffee warmed their hands.

"Been to the competition, have we?" She grinned at Gareth.

"I thought we should throw them a bone now and again."

Eleri choked on her pastry.

Gareth's eyes crinkled as they sank onto the sofa. Eleri treasured these quiet moments together. It soothed her nerves after the chaos of recent days. She felt ready to face whatever life was going to throw at her.

"Have you given any more thought to why we can't seem to leave town?" Eleri asked.

Gareth shook his head. "It was the strangest thing. But I did have an idea..."

Gareth moved closer on the sofa, taking both her hands in

his. His thumb caressed her knuckles, his expression earnest as their eyes met in a silent understanding.

"Eleri, what if we just get married?" he asked, his voice brimming with hope. "Make a proper life here, together."

Eleri's breath caught, his touch igniting a spark within her. She noticed him lean in, his handsome features just inches away.

"You must know how I feel about you," he continued, one hand releasing hers to tuck her hair behind her ear. "From the moment we met, I knew you were my soulmate."

His fingers lingered, tracing the line of her jaw. Eleri's pulse quickened at his sensual caress. Her lips parted as he tilted her chin up.

"We belong together, Eleri," he murmured, his smouldering gaze flicking to her mouth. "I want to build a future with you."

Eleri swayed closer, enthralled by the promise in his eyes. Her reservations faded, eclipsed by the desire blossoming inside her. Gareth's nearness left no doubt of his fervent feelings for her.

Eleri's breathing became shallow as Gareth moved closer, his expectant eyes searching hers. Her pulse drummed wildly in her ears, the room tilting around her. She dug her nails into her palms, trying to steady the dizzying rush of emotions. This was all happening too fast. Her mind reeled, unable to grasp the enormity of Gareth's proposal. It felt like just yesterday they were strangers from so many years apart, and now he wanted them to spend their lives together? It was overwhelming, like standing at the edge of a vast canyon with no way across. She had to slow down this careering moment before it swept her away. What if getting married made the curse worse?

Gareth pressed on. "Marry me, cariad. Let's face the unknown together, as husband and wife."

Overwhelmed, Eleri leapt to her feet. She paced to the window, staring unseeingly at the street below.

"Eleri?" Gareth's voice was filled with uncertainty. "I know it seems sudden, but in my heart, I've never been more sure of anything."

Eleri turned to him, tears glistening. "It's not that I don't care for you, Gareth. I just... I can't."

Gareth's face fell. "Why not?"

Eleri's fingers knotted in her lap as she struggled to find the words. How could she explain the maelstrom raging within? She cared for Gareth, she did, but accepting his proposal felt like jumping into the unknown.

"It's just...I..." she stammered, dropping her gaze. A dozen phantom rejections died on her tongue. She wanted to spare him pain, yet each halting attempt lanced her own heart with doubt.

Gareth leaned forward, urging her to continue. He looked so sincere. She saw a future brighter than any she had dared imagine. But the curse's shadow still loomed.

"I'm just not ready," Eleri finally managed. "Not yet." The admission wrenched free like a bone cracked from its socket. She searched Gareth's face, desperate for a trace of understanding amidst the heartbreak.

"I want to say yes. I honestly do. But everything is such a muddle right now, with the curse and not knowing what comes next. I can't make that kind of commitment until we understand what's happening."

She met Gareth's wounded gaze. "You have to see why I'm hesitating. I don't mean to hurt you, but..."

Gareth stood, shaking his head. "No, you're right. It was foolish of me. I got caught up in the moment."

He moved towards the door, but Eleri grasped his hand.

"What we have is special, Gareth. One day, perhaps..." she trailed off hopefully.

Eleri sank onto the sofa, distressed by the heartbreak she had caused him. Yet her reasons were sound - weren't they? A chill went through her as she recalled the book's ominous prophecy:

"Any union forged whilst the curse yet dwells will be doomed to fail."

Perhaps she had saved them from a bitter fate. Gareth's face crumpled, the light in his eyes extinguished. Eleri's breath caught at the raw pain in his features. Had she made the right choice? Her stomach twisted with uncertainty.

As Gareth turned numbly towards the door, Eleri wrapped her arms around herself. Long, lonely years stretched out before her if she let him walk away. Could she bear to lose his laughter, his warmth?

"Gareth, wait," she called out, her voice strained. He paused, a flicker of hope passing over his face. Eleri's heart hammered. She imagined throwing herself into his arms and whispering, "Yes."

But the cursed prophecy lingered at the recesses of her mind, holding her back. Gareth's shoulders slumped at her silence.

Gareth managed a sad smile. "I understand, Eleri. I just want you to be happy." He left without another word.

As the door clicked shut behind him, Eleri sank onto the couch, burying her face in a cushion. Had she just made the biggest mistake of her life?

Needing fresh air, she changed and set off towards the seaside. The briny breeze streamed over Eleri as she ambled along the promenade. Gulls cried out overhead, swooping and diving for scraps. Gripping the iron railing, she closed her eyes, letting the tangy air fill her lungs. When she opened them again, the sea glittered a brilliant sapphire, waves capped in ivory foam. She walked with lighter steps now, the heaviness of the morning's events fading with each step she took. The cry of seabirds and salt-kissed wind washed her spirit clean, leaving her freer than she'd felt in days. For the first time since the curse began, a smile came easily to her lips. Maybe this was the way to break the curse.

***

Turning into the alley's narrow street, Eleri stopped short as her aunt's. She smiled to herself. No, her bakery came into view.

As Eleri peered into the bakery's gloom, her attention was caught by a glint in the window of the abandoned shop next

123

door. An uneasy feeling crept across her, making her shiver. The air grew unnaturally still, as if the alley had been sealed in a vacuum. She inched closer, her breath pluming before her in wispy coils. The windows in the street darkened, driving her focus back to her bakery.

A spectre formed in the reflection, drifting nearer, a pale shimmer inside the cracked glass. Eleri's heart thundered as ghostly draughts swirled around her, carrying the faint scent of burnt sugar. Flickering shadows seemed to dance at the edges of her vision. The once-familiar bakery transformed into an eerie den.

"Aunt Ffion?" Eleri gasped.

Aunt Ffion's mournful face crystallised before her, more apparition than flesh. Eleri shuddered as those hollow eyes fixed on her, brimming with spectral tragedy. The phantasm's lips moved soundlessly; her message lost between worlds.

Icy fingers of dread gripped around Eleri's throat. Every instinct screamed to flee from the unnatural presence, but morbid fascination kept her feet rooted to the spot. She stood paralysed as the phantom dematerialised, darkness reclaiming the space where it once stood.

Eleri stared open-mouthed at the vacant shop. Gradually, the real world reasserted itself. Sunlight banished the darkness and gulls called. Had Aunt Ffion's ghost come to her, or was it an illusion woven by the curse? Eleri's pulse raced as she struggled to make sense of what she'd seen.

The spectre's mournful eyes haunted her, carrying some unfinished warning. Eleri's chest tightened, intuition whispering that Ffion's appearance was an omen. A reminder that death still lurked within the curse's shadows.

Shaken, Eleri backed away from the shop window. She thought of Gareth's earnest proposal, the longing in his voice. But her aunt's spectral presence reaffirmed her fears. Until the curse was broken, any attempt at forever could end in tragedy.

Wrapping her arms around herself, Eleri hurried onward. However much it pained her, refusing Gareth had been the right choice. She wouldn't bind him to an uncertain fate, no matter how her heart ached to do so. For now, navigating the curse alone was her burden to bear.

After collecting herself with a long walk along the breezy promenade, Eleri meandered back home. Pausing on her doorstep, she noticed a note tucked under the mat. In Gareth's handwriting, it read.

"I understand your doubts, cariad. My offer still stands - whenever you're ready."

Eleri clutched the note to her chest, overcome with emotion. Perhaps the curse dictated they must stay in Aberystwyth, but away from each other for now. But she knew without a shred of doubt that her heart belonged to Gareth, whatever happened.

Chapter 17

The smell of fish and chips spread from the pavement cafe along the harbour as Gareth shoved his hands into his coat pockets and walked along the promenade. Seagulls wheeled overhead, piercing the still morning air. The sunlight glinted off the Irish sea, casting everything in a reddish-gold early morning glow.

Autumn was over and an icy chill lingered on the breeze flowing in from the sea. He dug his chin down into his upturned wool coat's collar and continued trudging along the nearly empty pavement, keeping his head low and looking straight ahead to avoid making eye contact with the dog walkers. He wasn't in the mood for small talk.

Gareth understood her reasons - he really did - but it didn't make him feel any better. The wind whipped through his hair as he gazed out at the dark waters, wishing they could wash away his hurt.

Gareth tensed as he spotted John sauntering down from the other side of the pier towards him. His jaw jutted out and his fingers curled into fists at the sight of his old rival. Gareth scanned the area, contemplating ducking below the pier and hiding behind the cast iron supports to avoid any interaction. But John had already seen him, raising a hand in casual greeting.

With an inward sigh, Gareth forced his face into an impassive mask. His body tensing as John approached, dredging up memories better left forgotten - competing for Eleri's affection as teenagers, the bitter defeat when she chose John in the end. Gareth yearned to turn and walk away without a word. But his ingrained sense of courtesy wouldn't allow such blatant rudeness, no matter how much bile rose in his throat at the thought of making small talk with the man who once stole his dream of a life with Eleri.

Steeling himself, Gareth managed a curt nod in return as John stopped before him by the entrance to the Pavillion on the Royal Pier. Gareth focused on keeping his tone neutral, denying John an opportunity to glimpse just how unwelcome a blast from the past this meeting was.

"Fancy running into you here."

Gareth mustered a polite nod.

"Alright, John? I thought you'd gone back to London after you and Eleri..."

John waved his hand in the air. "Water under the bridge, mate. I'm just back in town, wrapping up some loose ends."

He leaned on the railing beside Gareth. "Let me guess - you confessed your feelings to Eleri, didn't you? I figured that was coming sooner or later."

Gareth bristled, not liking John's presumptuous tone. "My relationship with Eleri is none of your business anymore."

John held up his hands. "You're right, sorry. I shouldn't have pried." He was quiet a moment before continuing. "You're a good man, Gareth. Much better for her than I ever was. I truly hope you two find happiness together."

John's supportive words regarding his and Eleri's relationship made Gareth do a double take. Given their long and bitter rivalry for Eleri's affections, Gareth couldn't help but bristle with suspicion over this sudden change of heart. Was John just putting on a front to hide his true feelings? Gareth examined the other man, seeking any trace of persistent jealousy or insincerity. But John's expression remained open, his words sincere.

Still, doubt plagued Gareth. How could John simply let go of past resentment and wish them well so easily? There had to be some lingering bitterness over losing Eleri to a former rival. Gareth weighed his words before responding.

"I appreciate you saying that," he began. "But you'll have to forgive me for being sceptical. We have a complicated history, you, and me."

John nodded, looking thoughtful. "You're right, of course. I can't erase our past with a few words." He glanced out at the rolling waves. "All I can do is wish the best for you and Eleri now. I have found peace with how things turned out. What I felt was obsession. I know that now. I'm sorry."

Gareth studied the other man, looking for any hint of deception. But John's eyes remained clear, his words steady.

John shrugged. "Getting out of this town has given me perspective. Eleri was never going to be satisfied with an accountant. Aberystwyth is where she belongs." He smiled ruefully. "And I've realised I belong elsewhere. I'm off to America. Starting fresh."

"Well, good for you," Gareth said, meaning it. Perhaps John had changed after all.

Just then, Mary came bounding down the boardwalk. "John! I got us fish and chips." She handed him a parcel, then turned excitedly to Gareth.

"Gareth! You'll never believe it - John asked me to come with him to America. We're going to backpack across the country. Can you imagine?"

Gareth blinked in surprise as John slipped his arm around Mary. He had never imagined the two of them together. Mary's radiant smile as she stared up at John caused an unexpected shift in Gareth's perception.

Perhaps there was more depth to John than he'd given him credit for if he could make Mary so happy. He hadn't seen Mary for weeks at Eleri's.

Mary saw his confused expression. "John was coming into the hotel every morning for breakfast. I had to help mum and dad out. There's foot and mouth up at the farm and Nia couldn't get in. We just got chatting..."

Gareth observed the genuine affection between the unlikely pair with fresh eyes. For so long, he had resented John as a rival, blinded to any redeeming qualities. But knowing how long Mary had pined for John, even though she would never have admitted it, it seemed he must have matured into a man capable of being caring and devoted.

Watching John tenderly brush back a lock of Mary's windswept hair, Gareth felt an unfamiliar stirring of remorse over his harsh judgments. With this small gesture of intimacy, the years-long image of John as a callous heartbreaker began to crack and fall away. In its place remained just a man who had let himself discover a love worth embracing, just as Gareth had found with Eleri.

Perhaps they were not so different after all. The anger that had long simmered between them now cooled. John had moved on. With a thoughtful nod, Gareth, for the first time in years, thought of John as a friend rather than a rival.

Gareth's heart constricted. Hadn't he felt the same certainty about Eleri? He managed a smile. "I wish you both all the happiness in the world."

After quick goodbyes, he watched John and Mary stroll together down the promenade towards Constitution hill, their laughter floating on the breeze. Gareth sighed, envious but happy for them.

John had a point. Some people were wanderers at heart, while others thrived by putting down roots. Gareth knew Eleri was the latter. This little town shaped her into the person she was. Aberystwyth flowed through her veins as much as blood. She felt most herself wandering the cliffs where their aunt first showed her the constellations. This place nourished her soul. Gareth wouldn't dream of asking Eleri to leave, even as he didn't ache for broader horizons himself.

Standing alone on the windswept beach by the iron railing, Gareth felt his resentment toward John ebbing away. In its place, he felt compassion for two souls who had found love to guide them onward. He felt shame for the way he'd treated his onetime friend.

Gareth exhaled, the tension draining from his shoulders. There was no rush. He would wait patiently for Eleri to be ready. As long as they had Aberystwyth, and each other, they could weather any storm. Gareth smiled softly. He loved Eleri, and she was worth waiting for.

With these reflections bringing clarity, Gareth continued on his way, his steps feeling lighter. As he trudged up the narrow streets, the smell of frying fish and the sound of seagulls circling overhead blended into the familiar sensations of home. He would never leave. Aberystwyth was in his soul, just as Eleri was in his heart.

The thought of her brought a fresh rush of longing. Even with his newfound peace with John, Gareth felt impatience prodding at him. But the memory of Eleri's hesitance gave him pause. He would not rush her, no matter how his heart ached. She deserved time to lay her aunt's memory to rest before opening herself to new possibilities. His mind kept flitting from proclaiming his undying love to giving her time.

Gareth's feet carried him to the doorstep of Yr Wylan Fach, his favourite old pub. Suddenly craving the dim, wood-panelled interior he hadn't visited in ages. He pushed inside to find the familiar scent of smoked fish and whiskey enveloping him. He took a seat at the polished bar as the grizzled bartender nodded in recognition.

"Gareth boy, you're a sight for sore eyes," the old man rasped. "The usual then?"

"Please, Tom," Gareth said, settling onto the creaking barstool.

As Tom slid a pint of dark ale across the counter, Gareth let out a satisfied sigh. He had missed this place. He'd spent all his time lately at the bakery or the shop.

Gareth took a long draught, savouring the flavour. The pub's log fire cast shadows along the stone wall, creating a cosy atmosphere that relaxed his thoughts, inviting introspection. Gareth found his mind wandering back to his unexpected encounter with John.

Seeing John today dredged up old wounds Gareth preferred forgotten - the raw pain of Eleri choosing his rival still stung. But watching how John looked at Mary with unabashed devotion made Gareth reconsider. Even the arrogant kid who used to taunt him had grown into a man capable of loving someone.

Gareth took a long draw of ale, thinking. If reckless John could change, maybe it was time to let go of the grudge. Clutching their bitter rivalry brought nothing but bitterness. He had to stop living in the past.

The sting was fading. Gareth sighed, tension releasing from his shoulders. He'd carried the weight of this grudge for too long. It was time to forgive John and himself. The past was done. He should have fought harder for Eleri when they were younger, but the future remained unwritten.

As Tom quietly polished glasses nearby, Gareth stared into the swirling foam of his ale. He imagined his bitterness dissolving like sea foam, washed clean by the tides. For so long, jealousy towards John had tainted his memories of Eleri. But no more. The John he encountered today seemed a different man - content, caring, at peace with his choices.

Gareth realised with sudden clarity that he envied the liberation John had found. It wasn't anger anymore, but jealousy. While Gareth remained tethered to past wounds, John was free to seek new horizons.

A profound shift occurred in Gareth's spirit then. He felt the vice-like grip of resentment release within him. In its place, grew compassion for two people who had found an unexpected love, just as he and Eleri had.

The John of the past who had flirted with Eleri's affections was gone. In his place stood a man who knew what he wanted. Acceptance washed over him/ This town held a vitality and beauty that had kept him there, but there was always something missing. He realised that was Eleri. It was time he grew up, too.

Looking up from his swirling thoughts, Gareth noticed a white-haired old man sitting near the fire. His walking stick balanced against his chair arm. The man stared into his mug; weathered face lined with sorrow. Gareth wondered what regrets weighed on his soul.

Some pains could haunt a man his whole life, Gareth mused, if he let them. But like the tide, even the most persistent pains would recede if one waited long enough. All wounds could heal if given care and time.

Gareth glanced around the pub, seeing life carrying on even amidst the heartaches that touched every soul. The waitress laughed lightly as she carried dishes to the kitchen. Two drunks argued over football scores. A young couple gazed into each other's eyes in a distant corner.

The last of the tension released from his shoulders. The sea air sweeping through the open window carried with it a bracing clarity. He could waste no more time on the uncertainties of yesterday when the promise of tomorrow called.

Draining the last of his ale, Gareth set the empty glass on the counter with a satisfying thump. He bid Tom a good afternoon, then set off into the golden sunset with long, eager strides. Seagulls wheeled and cried overhead as he made for Eleri's flat, his footsteps light.

The breeze tousled Gareth's hair as he walked, carrying with it the scent of possibility. When he arrived on Eleri's doorstep, his heart quickened with anticipation. This time, when she opened the door, he would hold nothing back. He'd surrender his heart to her, allowing destiny to shape the happiness their connection could offer.

He arrived to find her kneeling in the back garden, hair escaping her braid as she tended Christmas roses. She was a beautiful picture.

Eleri glanced up, surprise flashing across her face before her expression softened into a smile.

"Those flowers are lucky to have you caring for them," Gareth said.

Pink tinged Eleri's cheeks. "Just trying to coax some colour back. Winter's been hard on them."

She stood, brushing the dirt from her dress. "I'm glad you're here. I hate how we left things."

Gareth took her hands. "I understand why you hesitated, and I don't want you to feel badly about it. I'm willing to wait for however long it takes."

Eleri's eyes glistened. "You're too good to me, Gareth."

He chuckled. "Hardly possible."

They shared a tender smile before Eleri led him inside. As they settled onto the sofa, she said, "I ran into John earlier."

Gareth arched an eyebrow. "What a coincidence. I bumped into him down by the harbour."

"Did he mention he was leaving town? And taking Mary with him?"

Gareth nodded. "He appears to have finally discovered his purpose. I suppose Aberystwyth was never a good fit."

"No, he was always too restless here." Eleri was quiet for a moment. "I'm glad Mary found love. She waited a long time."

Chapter 18

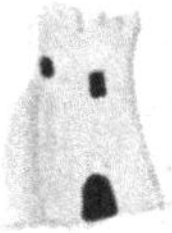

Eleri looked out of her flat window unseeing at the grey morning. She shivered despite her warm jumper, a sense of gloom settling over her. The weather seemed to match her mood.

They had scoured the scrapbook and ancient tome countless times for more clues about the curse's origins, but found nothing definitive. Did Cadwgan's wife curse Amelie for daring to claim her husband's love before she could? Was it his family trying to stop them marrying in the first place or was it Amelia herself, cursing her descendants because she could never have her true love? She couldn't imagine anyone being that bitter. It didn't matter how it started, if they didn't discover a solution soon, who knew what would happen? She'd never known her father. Did that mean Gareth was in danger? They had less than a month before Christmas Eve. It didn't feel long enough.

Eleri fidgeted anxiously with her locket as she watched workers stringing up glittering Christmas lights outside. She eyed the festive lights warily, each bulb seeming to tick off the days until their looming deadline. What usually felt like a countdown to her Christmas Day birthday was now a countdown to doom. She glanced worriedly up and down the street at the Christmas displays, a knot tightening in her stomach.

A knock interrupted her brooding. She opened the door to find Gareth, his crooked smile instantly lifting her spirits.

"Morning, cariad. Fancy a walk?" He offered his arm, which she gladly took.

They strolled hand-in-hand along the windswept seafront.

Slate grey waves churned under an equally stony sky. The cold air nipped Eleri's cheeks, making her grateful for Gareth's warmth beside her.

"I may have an idea about the curse," he said after they'd walked awhile. "What if we tried communicating directly with your ancestors? If we hold a ritual, their spirits might know something?"

Eleri bit her lip uncertainly. "I don't know if I could summon them."

Gareth gave her hand a reassuring squeeze. "You have a gift, Eleri. I know you can do this. The spirits are trying to talk to you. Maybe they will be clearer if you contact them on your terms."

"I'm not sure how," she confessed. "it's not like there's a school for this sort of thing. I've always just pushed them away."

Eleri hesitated, uncertainty clouding her eyes. But then she stood taller, holding her chin up with quiet resolve.

"Alright," she said, her voice steady with fresh conviction. "Let's try it."

That night, they prepared Eleri's flat. She lit candles throughout the space while Gareth drew the curtains and set out the scrapbook. They took their places on the rug, joining hands opposite each other.

Eleri took a deep, steadying breath as she glanced around the candlelit room. Shadows moved along the walls, lending an air of mystery. The sitting room seemed almost ethereal in the flickering glow.

She took Gareth's hands, meeting his eyes. He nodded encouragingly. Eleri closed her eyes and opened her mind, calling out into the void.

"Ancestors, please, I need your guidance and help right now." Her voice rang clear in the stillness. "Please, if you are there, give us a sign."

Only silence answered her summons. Eleri played with her hair as the quiet minutes crawled by. She could feel Gareth's hands warm in hers, the only sign this was not all some strange dream.

Eleri tried again, putting more force into her plea. "Dear ancestors, we need you! Help us break this curse before it's too late."

Again, no reply came. Doubt clawed at Eleri's mind. What if she didn't have the gift to reach them after all? She felt Gareth tighten his grip, bolstering her courage. She would try one last time.

"Ancestors of my blood, I know you can hear me," Eleri called out boldly. "As your kin, I ask you to appear and share your wisdom!"

A prickle raised the hairs on her arms as the room grew colder. Eleri's eyes flew open with a soft gasp. One by one, ghostly figures materialised before them, ethereal in the quivering candlelight.

Eleri's hand flew to her mouth as tears sprang unbidden to her eyes. Her grandmother and her great-aunts, generations of ancestors long passed, now stood silently observant. Each face was so achingly familiar, she could have picked them from a thousand.

Her grandmother drifted forward, eyes creasing in a kindly smile. "Dear child, we are here."

Eleri released a shuddering breath. "I've missed you all so much," she whispered. To see Nain again, after all this time, stirred such profound joy and sorrow, she could scarcely speak.

Gareth moved closer to her, so his arm circled her shoulders as Eleri gathered herself. She recounted their troubles with the curse and pleaded for anything that might help them break its power.

The spirits conferred in hushed murmurs before her grandmother addressed them. "All will become clear in time. For now, continue seeking the truth."

Frustrated, Eleri pressed for more help, but the ancestors remained vague and cryptic. As their forms began fading back into darkness, she cried out desperately, "Please, just tell us how to break the curse!"

Her grandmother's voice echoed around the room as the spirits vanished. "You already possess the means. Trust in your bond."

With those final enigmatic words, the candles extinguished themselves, leaving Eleri and Gareth alone once more in the moonlit room.

Eleri collapsed against Gareth's chest, emotionally spent. Her ancestors had dredged up feelings she scarcely knew how to articulate.

Gareth's arms enfolded her as she let the tears fall freely. He said nothing, simply holding her with steady patience until the storm of weeping passed.

Finally Eleri drew a shuddering breath and sat up, wiping her eyes with an embarrassed laugh. "Sorry about that."

Gareth cupped her face. "You've nothing to apologise for, cariad. I cannot imagine how difficult that must have been for you."

Eleri gave him a tremulous but grateful smile. Ever thoughtful, Gareth handed her a tissue and a glass of water from the side table. She sipped it, gathering her composure before speaking again.

"Well, that was rather pointless," Eleri sighed, thinking back to the ancestors' cryptic words. "We're no closer to any real answers."

Gareth pondered for a moment. "I don't know that I'd say pointless. At the very least, we now know the lockets must hold the key, as your grandmother said. Perhaps there is something hidden inside them."

He studied her face with concern. Dark circles smudged her reddened eyes, and fatigue weighed upon her delicate features. Pressing a kiss to her forehead, he said, "Don't lose heart, cariad. Just a few more days, and I believe this mystery will unravel."

Eleri tried for a tremulous smile, his presence renewing her worn spirits like a breath of fresh air. "I hope you're right," she murmured. With Gareth by her side, she could endure this a while longer.

Gareth rose and drew her to her feet. "Come now, let's get you to bed. Things will look brighter in the morning."

Eleri allowed him to guide her down the hallway, feeling the heavy mantle of exhaustion upon her. She climbed gratefully into bed as Gareth turned down the lamps and crept out of the flat.

Within moments, she slipped into a deep slumber, the image of her ancestors still imprinted behind her eyes. Though the ritual had not gone as hoped, seeing those beloved faces again was a gift Eleri would forever cherish. The rest would unravel in time.

The next evening, Eleri sat with Mary at her bakery, half-listening as her friend prattled on about her upcoming travels.

"California first, then maybe New Mexico..." Mary's eyes took on a dreamy cast. "Can you imagine road tripping with those roads that go on forever?"

Eleri's lips stretched tightly across her teeth in an imitation of a smile, even as her thoughts swirled elsewhere. She nodded along to Mary's stories, her responses on automatic.

A burst of laughter from outside caught their attention. Through the window, Eleri spotted Gareth chatting with a pretty tourist. The girl touched his arm, looking up at him adoringly.

Eleri's gut constricted, her strained smile faltering. She willed her lips to remain upturned, but the expression no longer reached her eyes. They stayed dark and troubled, her brows knitting ever so slightly.

She fidgeted in her seat, feigning interest in Mary's words while watching Gareth and the flirtatious stranger. Unease needled at her, despite her attempts to appear outwardly cheerful.

"Oh, I wouldn't fret about that, Leri," Mary said, noticing Eleri's preoccupation. "Gareth only has eyes for you."

She patted Eleri's hand reassuringly before launching into a story about her disastrous first driving lesson. But Eleri found it difficult to focus, watching Gareth laugh with the flirtatious outsider.

Gareth soon entered the bakery alone. "Ah, there are my two

favourite ladies." He kissed the top of Eleri's head. "Ready to head out, cariad?"

Eleri nodded, forcing a smile despite the unease still needling her.

"Just a moment." She shoo'd a laughing Mary out while kicking the door.

Later, she held onto Gareth's arm as they strolled home, trying to quell her irrational fears. Gareth was devoted - she had no reason to doubt his love.

As they passed a newsagent, Eleri's eyes were drawn to a newspaper stand displaying old headlines. She paused, an idea striking her.

"The photo!" she exclaimed. "The one in the locket with the young woman. I'll bet we could find out who she was if we checked the newspaper archives around the year 1916. She appeared quite young in that picture, so there may have been an engagement or wedding announcement printed."

Gareth's eyes lit up. "Brilliant idea! We already know she was the last person to wear the amulet from the inscription. Combing through the old announcements could give us a name and potentially more clues."

Eleri nodded, feeling a thrill of excitement. "First thing tomorrow, we'll head to the library and start digging through their newspaper records. I've a good feeling this could lead us somewhere."

Gareth grinned and hugged her, hope rekindled. "I knew you'd find the way forward, cariad. We're going to crack this curse yet!"

Chapter 19

Sunshine streamed through the library window where Gareth sat hunched over a computer screen. He scrolled through digital archives of old Welsh documents. After hours deciphering the handwriting, he finally found a match - Eleri's ancestor Carys Evans in the year 1893.

Now Gareth scoured the database for any mention of letters or records from that time period. The ancient microfiche equipment whirred and clicked as he skimmed through hundreds of files and documents. He didn't think they would ever digitise this stuff. Microfiche offered such an awkward bridge between the tactile feel of paper and the ease of computerised searches.

The library had a musty, aged smell from the tall stacks of physical books that surrounded the computer stations. Gareth took a moment to breathe in deep the scent of yellowing paper and worn leather bindings. It felt like home.

At last, he stumbled upon the announcements section of the Cambrian Mail in the archives. Gareth scanned the list of names on the grainy screen until he froze. There it was - Carys Evans, engaged to be wed to David Jones, proprietor. According to an 1893 entry, David Jones owned the general store on New Promenade at that time. The very building that now housed Gareth's own antique shop.

"Eleri, look!" Gareth waved her over excitedly. "I found your ancestor, Carys. She was engaged to a shopkeeper."

Eleri hurried to the computer, eyes widening as she read the faded digital entry.

"You found her! Oh Gareth, we need to learn more about her life." She jumped up, grabbing a stack of newspapers from that year. "Maybe the actual newspapers can tell us more."

They spent the next hours engrossed in century-old gossip columns and advertisements. Slowly, Carys Evans' world came into focus. She was the daughter of Iolo Evans. A socialite who had come up to Aberystwyth for her health and met David at the general store.

One editorial mentioned her homemade teas and tinctures using local herbs and plants. Gareth tapped the passage triumphantly. "A healer - just like you, cariad. Except you make people feel better with cakes." he winked.

Eleri smiled, eyes bright with wonder at this glimpse into her past.

The archive's clock chimed five. Gareth stretched back stiff from hunching over the table all day. "Shall we call it a night?"

Eleri didn't look up from her reading. "You go on. I want to dig a little deeper."

Gareth chuckled, kissing the top of her head before gathering his notes. Eleri was like a dog with a bone when she got fixated.

The next morning, he returned to find Eleri still surrounded by teetering stacks of records. Purple smudges under her eyes spoke of her all-nighter.

"Please tell me you eventually went home to sleep," Gareth said, only half-joking.

"Couldn't stop reading." Eleri grinned tiredly. "I learned so much about Carys' life. Did you know she ran a sewing evening for local women? And helped found a literary society?"

"How did you even get to stay in here? The librarian is a dragon."

"I'll tell her you said that. She's my friend from way back. Don't you remember her from Chemistry?"

"Not really, fach."

Her animated delight brought a smile to Gareth's face. He slid into the seat beside her with fresh coffee and pastries.

"Don't let her catch you with that Gareth, or she really will turn into a dragon!"

He ignored her. "You're amazing, you know that? Not

everyone would dive so deep into ancestor research so quickly. People usually need sleep." He teased.

Eleri glanced down as a flush crept up her neck at his words. She gestured to the sprawling collection. "I feel like I truly know Carys now. Her kindness, her curiosity and compassion..." Eleri's voice grew thick. "She reminds me so much of Aunt Ffion."

Gareth wrapped a comforting arm around Eleri's slumped shoulders. She hadn't smiled since she'd found out about the curse.

Finding this connection from the past meant a lot to Eleri, who deeply missed her aunt.

"Just think, cariad - you and Carys might be the only two to know about the curse," he mused. "I wonder if she recorded any details that could help us."

Eleri sat up straighter, re-energised. "Maybe she kept another diary? If it was kept by the library, it wouldn't be water damaged, like the scrapbook we found. They were super religious in those days. I've read they still arrested people they thought were witches until the 1940s. Making tinctures with herbal remedies would have pushed the limits - if anyone found that scrapbook they'd have crucified her. She would have hidden that scrapbook. But a normal diary... There could be one tucked away somewhere! I'll check the lists for any unidentified journals from that era."

Over the next weeks, they made little headway. No diary surfaced. But Eleri remained undeterred.

Late one night as rain lashed the windows of her flat, she gasped.

"Gareth!"

He jolted upright on the sofa to see her holding the locket with a trembling hand. "What is it?"

Eleri gasped, clutching the locket so tightly the edges dug into her palm. Carys' voice was as clear as if she stood beside her, whispering urgently in her ear.

"The floorboards... look under the floorboards..."

Eleri's heart thumped wildly in her chest. This couldn't be

real. But the voice echoed through her mind as clearly as if its owner stood right before her.

Eleri felt cold all of a sudden, shivering at the long-dead woman's presence. She had never felt such a raw, visceral connection to the past before. It was as if a ghostly hand had reached across the centuries to grab her.

Eleri's breath came in short, sharp bursts as she tried to understand this impossible situation. Carys Evans was speaking to her - imploring her - from beyond the grave.

The practical part of Eleri's mind rebelled at the sheer absurdity. Ghosts weren't real. This had to be some kind of hallucination brought on by stress and lack of sleep. Then she laughed at herself. That lack of sleep was getting to her. Hadn't she just spoken to her ancestors the other day?

The sincerity and urgency in the spectral voice gave Eleri pause. She could not shake the bone-deep certainty that this was indeed her ancestor's spirit reaching out across time.

Eleri turned, half expecting to see Carys' ghostly form behind her. But only empty air met her searching gaze.

"Carys?" Eleri whispered into the stillness. She wet her dry lips, voice quavering. "Is that you?"

The disembodied voice came again, now faint but unmistakable in its reply. "Yes, child...you must find the locket..."

Eleri's breath left her in a whoosh. Impossible as it seemed, she knew then this was a genuine message. Carys had somehow broken through and was guiding her descendant to unravel the curse's mysteries.

Eleri's mind reeled with the enormity of what was happening. She was communicating with a woman who had lived over a century ago! It seemed impossible, yet the spirit's presence was undeniable.

Gareth watched Eleri with concern. "What is it? What did you hear?"

"It was Carys," Eleri breathed. "She told me where to find the other locket - under the floorboards in your shop."

Gareth's eyes widened. They had scoured every inch of the

shop, to no avail. Could the ghost be right?

Eleri met his gaze, her own eyes blazing with exhilaration. "We have to go look right now!"

Gareth nodded, infected by her urgency. If this was true, it could be the breakthrough they desperately needed.

They rushed to his shop, where they took the steps two at a time up to the attic. They pried up floorboards, the rough splintered wood scratched against their palms, dust whirled up, attacking their nostrils in protest. Eleri winced as a splinter dug into her skin. The boards creaked and groaned in protest. They worked their way through the room until they struck a different type of wood - a hidden compartment! Heart pounding, Gareth lifted out what was inside. He grinned triumphantly; it was the other locket. Eleri bobbed up and down behind him.

"Is it there?"

Gareth handed Eleri the locket. Shuffling over on his knees so he could see it while she was examining it.

"There must be clues here about the curse's origins." She held the locket up to the bare light bulb. "Oh Gareth, now we can finally solve this mystery."

"Have you got the other locket on you?"

"Yes," her eyes gleamed. She handed back the locket he'd found while she ruffled about in her pocket.

They both held out the lockets until they touched. They held their breath, but nothing happened.

"Wh-a-a." Eleri's voice came out in a strangled wall.

"Give it here." He tried putting them together, but still nothing.

The lockets were identical. Tarnished silver with intricate Celtic knot designs on the front, with an oak leaf design on the back. He tried to open the new one, handing back Eleri's but it wouldn't budge. He frowned and awkwardly stood up, letting the blood flow back to his knees.

"I need to get some oil and maybe if we clean the metal up, we'll be able to make out some more detail."

She nodded and followed him downstairs. The main shop

was still boarded up, so he flipped the light to get a better look. He brought out a cloth from behind his counter and burnished the metal with it, adding some liquid from a can as he worked. Gradually, the silver gleamed under the light.

Eleri watched the engraving come to life under the burnishing, "They are beautiful."

"Why didn't you clean yours?" He asked as he smoothed the cloth along the chain.

"It's old. I didn't want to damage it. Or make things worse."

Next, he brought out the oil and squeezed the liquid onto the clasp, working it in with the cloth until it opened silently. They both leaned in. Inside was a picture that looked remarkably like Gareth.

"What the hell." He breathed. He leaned in, looking closer. They could make out the top of what looked like Victorian dress. "It looks like me." His voice trembled.

"Let me see." Eleri grabbed the locket. He was right. She stared at the picture, then at Gareth. It could only mean one thing. She opened her own locket and realised while it looked like Ffion, it looked more like her if she was honest with herself. "We must have lived before. Here. It must be the curse. We have to break it, or we'll be broken apart like them." She looked confused. "Or us? Before."

They spent the next hours poring over the locket, examining every minute feature. But no hidden buttons or compartments revealed themselves. Gareth's shoulders slumped. What were they missing?

"Maybe the answers aren't inside it," Eleri said. She held the locket up by its chain, watching it spin. "Could the metal itself be important?"

Gareth blinked, trying to shake off his exhaustion and grasping for this new lead through the fog in his mind. The locket seemed distinctive, with its braided chain and engraved knotwork...

He bolted upright. "The metal - that's it!" He grabbed the book, tracing the drawing. "Look here, these markings. This locket is no doubt Celtic, but I can't see anything else that differentiates it."

Eleri's eyes shone with dawning understanding. "Of course! That's significant, surely. The book mentions Celtic metalworking had mystical properties." She jumped up, pacing excitedly. "We need to take the locket to someone who knows old Celtic traditions who can help us access its power."

"Brilliant!" Gareth exclaimed. "I think I know just the person to help us."

***

At nine the next morning, they sat in Mr Evans' jewellery shop. Mr Evans hummed thoughtfully as he examined the jewellery, cleaning his spectacles on his worn cardigan dotted with holes. Despite his dishevelled appearance, he had a kindly spark in his eye.

"Fine Celtic craftsmanship here. My knowledge is a tad rusty, but let me see..."

He shuffled through drawers overflowing with trinkets until he found a massive magnifying glass. Gareth and Eleri exchanged amused glances as he held the giant comedic lens up to scrutinise the locket's engraving.

"Aha, just as I thought! See these interconnected knots? Represents the eternal love between you two." He shot them a playful wink.

Gareth rubbed his neck self-consciously while Eleri blushed.

"How do you know so much about Celtic artifacts?" Eleri asked.

The old man's eyes glazed with reminiscence. "I was quite the adventurer in my youth - traipsed all over the UK documenting occult objects. Had a real passion for the mystical."

His focus returned to the present. "I may have some ancient texts describing how to access the magic in these. Let me dig them up!"

He disappeared into the back room. Gareth and Eleri grinned as muffled crashes and inventive Welsh curses drifted out. Mr Evans soon emerged triumphantly clutching leather-bound tomes.

"My field journals! I knew they were here somewhere." He flipped through the pages excitedly. "Now let's unravel this mystery, shall we?"

Mr Evans tapped his chin. "Legends say these lockets held the spirits of ancestors, guiding the wearer through trials." He leaned forward, eyes twinkling. "Have you tried simply asking for aid?"

Eleri looked startled. "We did, but they were cryptical. They wouldn't give us any answers."

"They obviously wanted you to find the second locket. Maybe they couldn't tell you before? There are rules beyond the grave, like in real life."

"You think we should try again, with my ancestor, like before?"

The old man smiled. "Worth a try, eh?"

"There's nothing more about the lockets?"

"I'm sorry, but no. Only what I've told you. They are beautiful though, and ancient. I would go as far to say priceless."

After leaving Mr Evans' shop, Gareth and Eleri made their way to the misty seaside cemetery. Eleri clutched a bouquet as they walked among the weathered headstones.

When they reached the grave marked "Angharad Rhys, Beloved Mother," Eleri knelt on the damp grass. She laid the flowers down and traced her fingers over the engraved name.

"I wish you were here, Mam," Eleri whispered. A lump formed in her throat as she thought of her mother with her aunt Ffion. Both gone

Eleri felt Gareth's hand on her shoulder in silent support. After some moments, her trembling ceased as a sense of calm purpose flowed through her. Here, surrounded by her ancestors, Eleri felt closer to them than ever. She could almost hear their voices on the sea breeze, urging her onward.

Eleri rose and took Gareth's hand. Together they walked to the cliffs overlooking the crashing waves that held Ffion's spirit. Eleri closed her eyes, letting the salt-tinged wind wash over her. She drew strength from those she had lost. When the time came to summon Carys, their connection would help bridge the veil.

"I'm ready," Eleri said, resolve steeling her gaze. Hand in hand with Gareth, they left the cemetery and returned to his flat. After all, they'd found the second amulet there. They rushed around to prepare the ritual that would call forth Carys once more. Eleri carried her ancestors' love in her heart like a talisman lighting her way through the darkness. Carys wasn't there at the last ritual. Maybe she would be more forthcoming, especially as she was the one that had told them about the floorboards. Eleri clung to the hope.

As Eleri prepared the summoning ritual, a sense of foreboding filled the candlelit room. The flames flickered erratically, casting dark shadows on the walls, as she prepared to summon Carys' spirit.

Gareth watched anxiously, praying this attempt would finally reveal the answers they sought. Time was running out. He was inwardly fighting a storm of fear. This was all about Eleri before. Breaking a curse so he could be with her. Helping her to defeat the voices that plagued her. But that picture. He was involved now in a way he wasn't before. His image in Victorian dress kept floating in his mind. What did it all mean?

Eleri glanced up nervously as the single lightbulb overhead began to pulse and dim, then the candles winked out. "That's strange..."

Gareth frowned, rubbing his arms against the sudden chill in the air. "Is this normal? Should we stop?"

Eleri hesitated, then shook her head. "We must keep going. Carys is trying to cross over - we need to help guide her."

The temperature continued to drop until their breath came out in frosty puffs. Eleri's unease mounted, but she steadied her shaking hands and lit the ring of candles around the summoning circle.

A ghostly wind swirled through the room, making the candle flames gutter dangerously. Eleri's eyes widened as the locket began glowing with an unearthly light.

Gareth gripped her shoulder. "Are you sure about this?"

Eleri met his eyes, resolve steeling her nerves. "Yes. I can feel a presence - she's already here."

Right on cue, the lights cut out, leaving only the candles' eerie glow. Eleri took a deep breath and began chanting the ancient words given to them by the jeweller to complete the ritual. A distant rumble sounded, like a storm gathering its strength.

Gareth shivered as a ghostly figure materialised - a young woman in a long white gown, her hair in a neat braid.

At first translucent, the apparition solidified until the woman stood before them in ghostly detail.

Her skin, as pale as bleached bone, seemed to glow with a chilling inner radiance. Eyes that once were a startling green now shone silver like moonbeams. When she moved closer, her feet glided soundlessly over the floorboards.

The scent of dried lavender and oak moss emanated from her presence - echoes of the living woman she had once been. Her lips did not move, yet her musical voice reverberated through the room. It wasn't Carys.

"Please, help us..." Eleri implored.

The spectre's aura flickered as her phantom form wavered under the strain.

"Please, help us," Eleri implored again, swaying on her feet. "Tell us how to use the locket to break the curse."

The spectre hesitated, conflict in her eyes. When at last she spoke, her voice echoed as if from another world: "Mine is not to give the answer, but to guide thee to seek it within. Look within your own hearts. You need to correct a mistake I made."

As the spirit faded, Gareth caught Eleri's arm to steady her. Eleri slumped in disappointment, but Gareth gripped her hands, resolute.

"We're so close now, cariad. I know we can't see the way forward yet, but we will find answers. We have to."

Eleri managed a small smile. "I wish the woman had revealed

more. But you're right - we've come too far to give up hope."

Gareth tilted her chin up. "Hey, your optimism kept me going when I wanted to quit. Now it's my turn to remind you to have faith."

He pulled her into a fierce embrace. Eleri buried her face in his shoulder, drawing strength from his solid presence.

They stayed locked together as the first raindrops pattered against the window, each building with determination. The final battle against the ancient curse was approaching.

Chapter 20

The cold winter wind whipped Eleri's auburn hair across her face as she and Gareth hurried down the street toward her bakery in the centre of Aberystwyth. Despite the chill, she felt hopeful after their eventful morning searching for clues about the lockets. The decorations in the shop windows taunted her with the nearing deadline as they sped past.

Eleri unlocked the blue door to the bakery, the merry jingle of bells announcing their arrival. The rich, yeasty aroma of baking bread enveloped her, filling her with surprise and a comforting sense of home. She gave Gareth a grateful smile as she noticed the loaves proofing in the oven - he must have slipped in earlier to start the bread for her while she was distracted.

While Eleri busied herself rolling out fresh batches of Welsh cakes, Gareth wiped down the oak counters with a rag. Morning sunshine streamed through the bakery's picture windows, casting the oak seating in a cheerful glow. He clicked on the overhead pendant lights to brighten the displays of breads and pastries. Outside, residents bustled along the pavement down to the small town's high street, their voices drifting through the open door with the bracing scent of the sea. Seagulls wheeled and called as boats came in on the tide.

"What do you make of all this, then?" Gareth asked, leaning against the scrubbed wood counter as sun light spilled across its surface. His dark hair fell casually across his brow as he looked up at her, his brown eyes searching hers inquisitively.

Dusting the flour from her hands onto her faded apron, Eleri considered his question. Her brow furrowed. "I'm still trying to wrap my head around it all. The hidden compartment, the books, lockets...it feels as though we've unearthed more puzzles than answers."

She crossed her arms, rubbing away the ghostly chill that had gripped her upon touching the silver locket, its cold metal seeming to leach warmth from her bones. An inexplicable shiver ran down her spine despite the bakery's warmth. There was something unsettling, almost sinister, about the entire mystery that left her profoundly unsettled.

"Don't worry, cariad. We'll unravel this mystery yet," Gareth murmured reassuringly. His solid warmth was a calming influence among the fears swamping her thoughts.

Eleri managed a wan smile that didn't reach her troubled eyes before busying herself with tidying the already spotless counter, trying in vain to ignore the squirming unease twisting her stomach into knots. The spectre of Aunt Ffion, and the secrets she seemed determined to reveal from beyond the grave, still lingered at the edges of Eleri's mind, refusing to grant her peace.

A couple hours later, Mary breezed into the bakery, her blonde hair windswept and rosy cheeks flushed from the bracing sea air.

"Bore da!" she sang out cheerfully, the shop bells chiming her arrival. "I come bearing savoury gifts from the shores of Borth."

With a flourish, she held up a hand-woven basket brimming with freshly baked crusty bread still warm from the oven, wax-wrapped chunks of creamy Welsh cheese, and other delicious delicacies brought from her parents' seaside hotel. The tangy, comforting scents instantly lifted Eleri's mood.

"Ooh, brilliant, you are a treasure!" Eleri exclaimed, giving her friend an impulsive, one-armed hug before eagerly poking into the full basket with the other.

"What's this?" She held up a small baguette, waggling it in front of Mary's nose in mock horror. "I see you didn't think my baking was good enough, having to nick bread from your parents' kitchens. No matter, I'll just have to whip up something extra delicious to regain your loyalty," she added with a playful wink.

Mary laughed, unfazed by her friend's teasing. "Oh, come now, you know you can't beat your bread fresh from the oven. But I simply couldn't deny my parents the pleasure of sending you a gift. Even if they don't realise, they're doing it," she said.

"Besides," Mary added, lowering her voice conspiratorially, "don't let it go to your head, but your Welsh cakes are still my favourite treat in all of Aberystwyth." She shot Eleri a wry smile. "Just don't tell my parents," she added in an exaggerated whisper.

"So how was your weekend?" Eleri asked.

"The beach was glorious as always," Mary replied breezily, unpacking the bounty onto the worn oak counter. "It was so lovely to get away before things get truly mental with the Winter Fair next week. Speaking of which, have you finalised your show-stopping recipe for the bake-off yet?"

Eleri hesitated, her stomach sinking. Between running the bakery and investigating the curse, she'd hardly had a moment to ponder what creation she'd unveil for the competition.

Noticing her telling pause, Mary gave her a playfully stern look. "You'd better get cracking, Eleri fach," she tutted, eyes glinting mischievously. "We can't have Cafe Eleri's booth sitting empty during the fair's highlight event now, can we?"

Eleri nodded absently. The scrapbook waiting in the cupboard upstairs called to her. Maybe she hadn't checked it out closely enough? But the Winter Fair required her full attention - it was her opportunity to showcase her recipes and bring in customers during the slow winter months. She pushed thoughts of the book aside; it would have to wait.

At that moment, the bells above the door jingled sharply. Eleri glanced up to see John stride in, cheeks ruddy from the cold. Her heart stuttered in surprise. What was he doing here? His eyes met hers briefly before skittering away.

"Alright, Eleri?" he asked, a little too casually, running a hand through his artfully tousled blond hair. The familiar gesture twisted her heart.

"Fine, thanks," she managed crisply, busying herself behind the counter to hide her sudden discomposure. The warm bakery air seemed to thicken with tension. She noticed Mary fidgeting out of the corner of her eye.

"Cake?"

John shook his head. "No thanks, just popping in for a quick hello. Meeting some mates at the pub soon." He shuffled his feet, gaze fixed on the floorboards.

"Hello," Eleri replied evenly, guarding her tone. She knew he was with Mary now, but years of history couldn't be casually erased like that. She must have loved him once. Was he over her, as he claimed? She studied his face, searching for any hint of lingering affection. But his eyes were guarded, revealing nothing.

Eleri straightened up decisively, smoothing her apron. Time would tell if he still had any feelings for her, but for now, she would take him at his word. She turned to Mary with forced brightness. "Mary, we've found both lockets! I'll just go grab them from upstairs."

"Aunt Ffion's locket?"

Eleri shook her head. "No, I don't believe either locket belonged to Aunt Ffion - at least not for a long time. I found one washed up on the beach months ago and Gareth and I discovered the other one hidden under the floorboards at the back of Gareth's shop. Hang on a minute, let me just grab them from the flat."

Eleri hurried to the back as Mary smoothly stepped in. "Right then, while Eleri retrieves the lockets, anyone fancy a mug of tea?" she offered breezily.

"That would be lovely, thank you," Gareth replied with an appreciative smile.

"I'd love a cuppa," John chimed in, seeming to relax.

"Coming right up!" Mary's slim form breezed through the door into the cafe kitchen, her cheerful humming fading as it closed behind her.

Gareth shifted awkwardly in the sudden silence left in Mary's wake. John busied himself peering at artwork hanging on the bakery walls.

Eleri came bounding down the stairs, her excitement evident in her energetic movements. But when she reached the doorway, her eager expression faltered at the sight of John and Gareth's tense body language. "Is everything okay?" she asked uncertainly, glancing between the two men.

"Yes, fine," John muttered, avoiding her eyes.

Gareth settled on the stool beside John and nodded at him politely. An awkward silence descended.

Without a word, Eleri set a faded blue diary on the counter with a gentle thud.

John squinted at the diary. "Is this... Ffion's?"

Eleri nodded, her mouth abruptly dry. "I just found it in the office. It fell off the shelf. I thought it was just another accounts book, but when I opened it..." she explained once she found her voice again. "As for the locket, it washed up on the beach one day." This was ridiculous. She didn't need to keep reminding him where she got the bloody locket from, but the way he'd reacted before, she couldn't help herself.

She swallowed hard, steadying herself before continuing. "I thought - hoped that there might be something important inside. Some answers that Ffion meant for us to uncover."

Eleri paused, releasing a trembling exhale. "Something she would have wanted us to see," she finished quietly.

She hesitated, then added in a rush, "I've been seeing Ffion's ghost. She's trying to warn us about something." It was a relief to confess it openly now that John no longer felt like her enemy.

Reverently, she opened the diary's cover. Her eyes misted as she traced a finger over Ffion's looping script.

Eleri cleared her throat and read aloud.

"November 10th, 1995. The winter fair is tomorrow night. Eleri doesn't know it yet, but I've made her a costume for the costume parade..."

The comforting scents and warmth of the bakery faded as Eleri's eyes glazed over the diary's faded pages. The cheery interior melted away into a blur of twinkling lights and looming shadows.

Thick snow blanketed the frozen ground, glittering under the pulsing lights of rides, game, and clothes stalls. Highly unusual by the seaside, the snow muffled the tinny music echoing eerily through the busy funfair. No new flakes fell, just the heavy layer already coating the stalls and icy pavement.

Ffion looped her bright red wool-clad arm through the younger Eleri's for balance, guiding each other down the icy lane between stalls as their feet slipped their way along. The scents of popcorn, roasted nuts and mulled wine mingled in the freezing air. Teen Eleri gazed up in wonder at the looming Ferris wheel, its rainbow lights diffused through the heavy snow coating the ground.

Her boots crunched and slid over the snow-blanketed pavement as music and laughter echoed around the stalls. She paused at a distorted mirror at a game stall, seeing her round, wind-nipped 14-year-old face staring back, framed by the furry hood of her cobalt coat.

Eleri watched her younger self through the mirror, feeling the bitter cold seeping through her own ghostly form encased in her younger self. She could smell the sweets and wine, hear the music - yet she was just an observer here, a passenger in this frozen fragment of the past.

Gareth and John's footprints trailed behind in the thick snow, their elbows jostling for Eleri's glancing attention. Ffion led them toward the red and green lights of the spinning Ferris wheel, cutting through the night sky. Eleri hesitated, glancing back at the eager faces of the boys behind her, their outlines blurring as the memory dissolved.

Young Eleri hesitated, glancing back uncertainly at the two eager faces behind her, their features blurring as the memory faded.

Eleri blinked, finding herself abruptly back at the counter in the bakery, the diary slipping from her trembling fingers onto the worn countertop with a dull thud. For a moment, she didn't move, the ghostly scent of mulled wine and sweet popcorn mingling with the familiar aromas of the bakery.

Eleri's mind reeled as she tried to make sense of what had just happened. She looked up to see John and Gareth sat on stools in front of her, equally stunned, eyes wide. "You both saw it too, didn't you? The fair. We were actually there."

John nodded; his brow furrowed. "It was like being inside one of Ffion's memories, our memories. That night, when you and I dated for the first time." He trailed off, leaving the recollection unfinished.

Eleri's thoughts raced as she gripped the diary again with trembling hands. There must be something more here, some unfinished business or hidden message from her aunt.

The sickly sweet scent of candied apples mingled with popcorn returned as Ffion led young Eleri toward the garishly lit Ferris wheel. Eleri glanced back uncertainly at Gareth and John trudging through the heavy snow on the edges behind them. The boys' raucous laughter belied the simmering tension as they vied for her childhood affections.

Shy Mary lingered in their wake, doe eyes fixed longingly on John's profile as he jostled and joked with Gareth. Eleri clutched Ffion's arm, a dawning unease settling in her stomach. She realised with sudden clarity that her choice tonight would ruin both couples' chances for love.

Young Eleri saw only John, spellbound by his roguish crooked smile and the way his glance made her heart flutter. Blind to Gareth's steady devotion, she was intoxicated by John's fun-loving personality. Oblivious to the raw pain in Gareth's eyes, she walked away on John's arm, giggling at a joke.

Eleri split from her younger self, standing apart, Gareth and John floated away from their younger selves to stand beside her, watching the enfolding scene. Regret held the adult Eleri captive, rendering her motionless. Now she saw the depth of Gareth's love, so recklessly abandoned that night. If only she had recognised his devotion rather than discarding it so thoughtlessly in the snow. Perhaps she could have made a different choice. The diary slipped through Eleri's trembling fingers, questions swirling as the memory faded, bringing her back to reality.

Eleri's throat constricted. She'd been only fourteen that night when she chose John's infectious laughter and daring spirit over Gareth's steady companionship. Too young to grasp the consequences. What might have happened if she'd chosen differently? Could she have known her choice would lead John to become a miserable accountant, crushed in spirit by years in London, trying to provide for her? Guilt suffused Eleri's thoughts as she wondered if she had altered the course of John's life by choosing him. If only she could go back and make a different decision. Their lives would be so different now.

Gareth was watching her closely, a questioning look in his eyes. Her heart fluttered under his patient gaze.

Eleri placed Ffion's diary back on the counter, hands trembling with regret. As she did, the two silver lockets clinked together, piercing her heart. She stared at the engraved pendants, knowing they represented the lives she'd ruined with her choice years ago.

Eleri gripped the lockets tightly. She had a lot of thinking to do. But first—she turned and caught Gareth's eye, managing a tremulous smile—there was a present to untangle.

Mary reappeared just then, bearing a laden tea tray. "Right, who wants biscuits? Anyone?" She glanced between them quizzically.

"What did I miss?"

Chapter 21

The memory faded, leaving John staring down at the open diary on the bakery counter. A smile crept across his face as Mary's image lingered in his mind. He had noticed her in the memory, quietly standing by the ghost train as he and Gareth vied for Eleri's attention. He hadn't seen her then, but he did now.

Mary was all he could think about. Her patience, her gentle spirit, her unwavering love - she was his lighthouse. Guilt washed over him for taking so long to see her. But no more. That memory took away any doubts.

John took a deep breath as Eleri closed the diary across the cafe counter, resolving to make things right. He looked up to see Mary bustling around the bakery, her kind eyes crinkling as she helped customers who must have come in while they were in the memory. It felt like half an hour had passed, but it must have been moments. Even in her work apron, with her hair falling from its bun, she was beautiful to him.

"Mary, do you have a moment?" John asked.

Mary's eyes widened in surprise. "Of course." She untied her faded apron and came around the wooden counter, her shoes clicking on the tile floor.

He clasped her hands in his, meeting her curious blue gaze. "Seeing you in that memory...it made me realise what an idiot I was when we were kids. You were always there, but I didn't see you properly. You've always been there for me, but I was too foolish to see it. I'm so sorry, Mary. Can you forgive me?" His voice cracked on the last words as his thumbs caressed her knuckles.

Mary studied his face for a moment before a small smile

crept onto her lips. "Of course, I forgive you, John," she said. "I know you didn't mean it."

John let out a shaky breath as Mary's words washed over him. Gratitude shone in his eyes, brimming with emotion. Her hands felt soft in his, and he relished their warmth. He finally saw the woman before him - her patience, her grace, her unwavering loyalty.

Mary gazed up at him, her blue eyes glistening. "Oh John, you're already forgiven. I hoped one day you'd see me, even when you were distracted." She gave a watery laugh. "Distracted is an understatement for you."

John chuckled ruefully and pulled her close, one hand moving to caress her cheek. "You're absolutely right, as always. But not anymore. From now on, I promise you'll be first in my heart."

He dropped to one knee, never breaking eye contact. "Mary Jones, will you make me the happiest, most blessed man in Wales by consenting to be my wife?"

Mary's hand flew to her mouth, tears spilling down her cheeks. "Oh John! Of course, yes!" She threw her arms around him, laughing and crying at once. John held her tight, tears of joy pricking his own eyes. He had finally found his way home.

Eleri emerged from the kitchen. John apologised to her as well. Eleri forgave him warmly.

John swept Mary into an ecstatic kiss. When they finally broke apart, breathless and flushed, he kept his hands clasped in hers.

"I don't want to wait. How would you feel about having the ceremony on Christmas Eve?" he asked. "We could exchange our vows surrounded by all the books you love so much at the National Library, with Eleri making a Yule log cake as our wedding pudding."

Mary's eyes shone. "It sounds absolutely perfect!"

As they embraced again, Eleri bustled over with a tray of gingerbread men. "Did I hear wedding plans? I'd be honoured to bake a cake for your special day!"

The three friends smiled joyfully, caught up in the excitement of the future unfolding before them.

*****

Over the next week, jealousy pricked Eleri's heart as John and Mary visited the library to reserve the gallery for their Christmas Eve ceremony.

Mary spread out sample invitations on the bakery table as Eleri brewed a pot of tea. "What do you think of these simple cream ones with the floral border?" Mary asked.

Eleri clasped her trembling hands under the table so Mary wouldn't see. She took a deep breath and steadied her voice. "They're perfect. The guests will love them."

Mary beamed. "Great! Now help me address them?" She slid a stack of envelopes across the table, dividing them into three. Giving one set to Eleri and one to John. With a weak smile, Eleri picked up a pen, but the oven timer went off. She popped behind the counter to empty the oven, still listening to her friend. Writing out envelopes was a stinging reminder of the wedding she'd never have.

"I was thinking string quartet to go in," Mary mused as she worked. "Then a harpist for the cocktail hour."

Eleri nodded, her throat tightening. She'd always imagined walking down the aisle to a romantic piano melody. She blinked as her eyes misted over, focusing on the brownies in front of her.

"Ooh, and I found the perfect reading," Mary continued, describing the ceremony details that echoed painfully in Eleri's heart.

Eleri painted on a smile, pushing down her grief to share in her friend's joy. If only wedding planning didn't sting so bitterly, she thought, blotting a fallen teardrop so Mary wouldn't notice. If they couldn't break the curse, at least she could swallow her sorrow and help make Mary's wedding wishes come true.

Eleri nodded along, even as she ached for what could never be with Gareth. She swallowed her pain and focused on supporting Mary, ignoring the spear of envy in her chest.

A week before the wedding, Mary rushed into the bakery, flushed with panic. "The bridal shop just called - they had a cancellation for a fitting on Christmas Eve morning. It's the only time I can get in to find a dress off the rack!"

Eleri pasted on a smile. "That's brilliant, cariad! We'll make sure you get there on time."

Inside, her heart felt tight. While Mary scrambled to get ready on her wedding day, Eleri would mourn dreams that could never come true. But she would swallow her sorrow to help her dear friend find the perfect gown, even if she wished the appointment was her own.

Chapter 22

The boutique's window displayed a collection of elegant gowns in gorgeous silks and fine French lace. Inside, racks of dresses lined the pink damask walls. Crystal chandeliers cast a warm glow on the polished wood floors.

Madame Dupont emerged from behind a velvet curtain, her nose in the air. "What is your vision for the day, my dear?" she asked Mary. Eleri held up a beaded gown, but the woman didn't so much as glance her way, keeping her attention fixed entirely on Mary. "And of course, your budget?" the woman asked in a haughty tone.

Madame Dupont continued speaking to Mary as if Eleri wasn't there. Perplexed, Eleri moved directly in front of the woman and waved the dress right in her face. "Hello? I have a dress here!"

With a sniff, Madame Dupont looked her friend up and down and continued to address Mary. "Shall we begin the fittings?"

In the plush dressing room, Mary shimmied into a sleek red gown with a plunging neckline. She stepped out shyly for Eleri to see.

"Wow!" Eleri whistled. "You look fab!"

Mary laughed and did a little twirl. Madame Dupont looked aghast.

"Heavens, that's far too scandalous for a bride your age," she scoffed.

Next, Mary tried on a conservative high-necked dress with long lace sleeves. Madame Dupont nodded in approval, but Mary frowned at her reflection.

"I look like someone's nana," she complained.

"Don't settle," Eleri insisted. "This isn't the one either."

Finally, Mary emerged in a classic white A-line gown, simple yet elegant. Eleri gasped, hands flying to her mouth.

"Oh Mary, you look absolutely stunning!" Eleri gasped.

Mary glanced at herself in the mirror, her eyes distant.

Eleri frowned. "What's wrong? Don't you like it?"

"It's beautiful," Mary murmured. Her eyes drifted to the corner of the room where a crumpled newspaper lay. Mary picked up the discarded paper, her fingers tracing the worn edges. Half the page was adorned with a photo of Eleri, her face taken from a Friendface post, juxtaposed with an image of a mangled campervan.

"Why does this paper say you died in a car crash six months ago?" Mary asked, meeting Eleri's eyes in the mirror.

Eleri's breath caught in her throat. She joined Mary by the mirror, hands trembling as she took the paper.

Dread crept up her back. With trembling hands, she reached for the paper, staring down at her own picture. Was that her campervan? A horrific car crash... her campervan veering off the coastal road to Aberystwyth...

The white dresses lining the walls of the boutique blurred as Eleri's mind drifted. She found herself in her van, screeching tires piercing the air. She jerked the wheel left, trying to avoid the oncoming car. Her campervan fishtailed, the guardrail flying past in a grey streak. The front wheels left the pavement, tires spinning over thin air. Eleri's stomach lurched as the van plunged over the cliff's edge. A deafening crash of shattering glass and crunching metal drowned out her scream. Then, blackness.

Eleri grasped Mary's hand, desperately seeking an anchor among the swirling revelations. "I'm... I'm dead?"

Confusion clouded Mary's expression, but then her face contorted in realisation, the truth dawning upon her. She nodded solemnly, taking hold of the paper, scanning the article. She looked into Eleri's eyes, her blue eyes pooling with sympathy as she placed it down once more. "There was an accident. You didn't make it."

As the words left her mouth, real understanding dawned on Mary's face. She glanced around the boutique, taking in the too-bright lighting, the flawless dresses. With a trembling hand, she reached for the newspaper on the chair again.

27-YEAR-OLD WOMAN KILLED IN CLIFF CRASH, the headline declared. Mary's eyes scanned the article, filling with tears as she took in the date - six months ago. The photo showed Eleri's mangled campervan on the rocks below the sea cliff.

"Oh Eleri," Mary breathed. "I remember hearing about a crash, but I didn't know it was you. I'm so sorry."

Eleri swayed on her feet. The boutique seemed to spin around her. She couldn't be dead. Just this morning, she had laughed with Mary over coffee. But the evidence stared up from the newspaper's stark black and white print. She looked at her hands. They were translucent, like she was fading in and out.

"Why am I here? How can you see me?" Eleri finally managed.

Mary set down the paper, fresh resolve settling on her features. "I think ... I think we're not ready to let go. But we'll figure this out together." She went to clasp Eleri's hand, but they went through them.

The truth crashed over Eleri in crushing waves. She hasn't been here all this time helping her dearest friend. She died that day on the cliffs six months ago. Which meant...

"Gareth!" Eleri exclaimed. "I have to get to Gareth!" Without thinking, she sprinted from the shop. Buildings and landscapes blurred past in a swirl of motion and emotion.

The cheerful bell above the door jangled as Eleri stepped into the bakery. Her breath caught at the sight. Gone were the lively colours she had painted the walls. No tempting aromas of fresh bread and pastries filled the air. Dust layered the empty display cases like snow.

Eleri drifted through the abandoned shop in disbelief. Everything they worked for was gone, all their dreams they'd poured into this place. Long nights baking together, flour coating their faces and laughter coating their hearts. Had it all been an illusion?

At the back, Eleri halted before the kitchen door. She could almost hear sounds from the past few months - the whir of the stand mixer, the scrape of wooden spoons on bowls. With a deep breath, she pushed open the door.

The kitchen stood dark and lifeless. No proof remained of the memories that felt so real in her mind. Eleri sagged against the wall, grief rising in her throat.

"Gareth!" she called out, desperate and broken. Only silence answered her cry.

This place, these dreams - it was everything. But in truth, she was alone. Eleri sank to the floor, heart shattered. She had never baked with Gareth, never decorated with him or built a life here. That future died on the cliffs with her.

Eleri wept for all she had lost. The sting of death sunk into her soul. But finally, she rose with steely resolve. If this was all an illusion, she would no longer cling to it.

At first, only silence answered her. Then, faint footsteps approach. Gareth's translucent form comes into view, his eyes widening when they met Eleri's.

"Eleri? Is that you?" Gareth's voice cracked with emotion as he drifted towards her.

Eleri rushed to embrace him, but her arms passed right through his spectral form. Tears spill down her cheeks. "Oh Gareth, I'm so sorry! I didn't know... I didn't know I was dead!"

Gareth's ghostly hand reaches out as if to wipe her tears away. "It's okay, my love. I didn't realise either until it was too late. Mary just came to the shop."

Eleri followed as Gareth's spirit glided away, leading her down the street to his antique shop. Or rather, what remained of it. The smart storefront had been reduced to a blackened shell, smelling of smoke and loss. The window vandalised in the months since.

"There was a fire," Gareth said numbly. "It ripped through while I was working late one night. I tried to get out but..."

He blinked, and Eleri saw it. Black smoke surrounded them.

Gareth's eyes widening in fear. He spun on his heel to flee the fiery blaze overtaking the room, but stumbled over a fallen beam. Flames licked at his legs as he struggled to his feet. Panicked, he limped towards the exit, coughing, and gasping through the thick smoke. He made it just a few steps before crumbling to the ground. Within seconds, the ravenous fire engulfed his body.

"All I could think about was you," Gareth continued, his voice breaking. "I hadn't seen you for ten years, yet ... I was thinking about how I'd never see you again."

Tears ran down Eleri's cheeks, hands clasped over her heart. "I'm here now."

But as they hold each other in their grief, the truth remained - their lives were over, leaving them as ghosts clinging to their lost dreams. The living must carry on without them.

They went back to the café, and sat there for hours until the late afternoon pale winter sun filtered through the frosted windows, casting a soft glow on the couple seated at the corner table. Gareth shifted in his seat. His voice was low and urgent.

"Eleri, John and Mary are to be married tonight. Would you marry me at the same time? Obviously not during their ceremony, that wouldn't be right, but we could marry straight after. Our friends will be there. If we are to be separated forever tonight, then at least we can be together when it happens."

Eleri searched his face and then grinned.

"Yes, but won't it steal Mary's thunder?"

Gareth took Eleri's hand in his own. "You know, it was actually Mary's idea to have the wedding with them," he said. "I was thinking something a little different - a beach ceremony, with the wind whipping through our hair as we exchanged vows in the rain."

Eleri laughed and nudged Gareth's shoulder. "Oh sure, because having all our guests soaked and freezing during the ceremony sounds ideal!" she teased.

"What says Aberystwyth, more than rain?" Gareth clutched his chest in mock affront. "You wound me!" he cried. "But truly, I cannot wait to marry you, rain or shine. Though I admit the library will make a great romantic backdrop for our special day."

Eleri smiled, leaning in to give Gareth a quick, tender kiss. Gareth smiled as he reached across to take her hand. His rugged features softened in the morning light.

"Eleri," he said. "Just think, tonight you'll be my wife."

Eleri's grinned. After realising they were both ghosts trapped between worlds. Whatever happened, they had found a sort of peace. They still had until midnight until the curse would do what it would. At least she could have her last wish. It wasn't what she envisioned, but being married to Gareth was what she wanted.

The tinkling of the front door pulled Eleri from her thoughts. She looked up to see Mary breezing in, cheeks flushed from the winter chill outside. Her blonde hair curled around her shoulders as she unwound her scarf.

"Afternoon, you two!" Mary chirped, plopping down in the chair opposite them. "Got your dress yet? You've only a few hours!"

Eleri smiled wryly at her friend. "Still working out the details for my ethereal gown. Might be a bit tricky to find the right ghostly look."

Mary laughed, her blue eyes twinkling. "Well, at least I know all my guests will actually be able to see me in my dress. Silver linings, right?" Her tone was subdued. "I'm sorry Eleri. It's not the ideal way to marry your true love."

Soon, customers started trickling in, drawn by a sudden scent of fresh pastries and coffee. Eleri looked up, confused.

"Ah Cariad, you wouldn't have been able to serve the living," said Mr Pritchard, standing first in the queue. As she watched, he grew younger. "You have control over how you look and your surroundings. Try it."

Eleri looked at the dirty, neglected room. She could change this? But she took him at his word and willed the bakery to transform into how it was. Suddenly, the colour of the walls transformed, and the dust disappeared.

Mary laughed in the corner. "I wish I could do that."

Mr Pritchard grinned at Mary. "I've been worried about you, girl. Ghost pastries don't have calories, you've lost a lot of weight, cariad. We would have had to do an intervention if you'd got any slimmer, but you'll make a beautiful bride, regardless. John is a lucky man."

"He is, isn't he?" Mary grinned back. Catching sight of her phone on the table, she saw it flashing. "I have to go get ready for the wedding. Mum is back at the hotel waiting. See you at the wedding?"

Everyone nodded and Mary laughed add she almost skipped out.

Eleri busied herself behind the counter, chatting warmly with the locals. Who knew that all the customers had been ghosts?

An hour later, Eleri stood gazing out at the sea as icy waves crashed on the shore. She drew her cardigan tight against the biting wind.

Strong arms encircled her, and she leaned back into Gareth's embrace. "You're miles away, cariad. What's troubling you?"

Eleri sighed. "Just thinking about Ffion. We can see all the other ghosts now, but I haven't seen Mam or Ffion."

Gareth nodded, his stubbled chin brushing her hair. "I understand. Maybe you need to call them? They may be holding back for some reason."

"Call who?" a warm voice came from behind them and Ffion was there.

"Ffion! I've missed you."

"I'm sorry, cariad. I couldn't tell you that you were dead. It's the rules of the curse. We usually help each other as soon as we die, but the curse prevented that with you. I tried to break through. Every time you pushed each other away, I tried to warn you. It was funny watching you try to leave Aberystwyth, though. You can't leave the place you die in."

"We know that now." Eleri laughed.

"It's time to get ready, dear." She turned to Gareth, "go off now, decide what you are going to wear for your wedding."

Ffion smiled warmly at her niece. "Come now, let's get you

ready!" She led Eleri back inside the café.

"I know you can't have a physical dress, but as a spirit you can manifest whatever outfit you desire," Ffion explained. She urged Eleri to close her eyes and focus.

Eleri pictured a simple but elegant lace wedding dress and flowing veil. She felt a tickling sensation and opened her eyes to see the spectral gown shimmering around her.

"Oh Eleri, you look beautiful!" Ffion said proudly. "Your mam would have been so happy to see this day."

At the mention of her mother, Eleri felt a pang of sadness. "Do you think she's moved on?" she asked.

Ffion nodded, a knowing look in her eyes. "I believe so. That's the natural way of things. But she'll be watching over you always, as will I. She wasn't a direct descendant of Amelie, like us."

"Can you tell me more of the curse?"

"It still binds us, child. We are free to talk about your death because you found out yourself, but anymore..." She held out her arms in apology.

Eleri hugged her aunt, comforted. She was ready now to marry her beloved Gareth, whatever happened tonight, surrounded by both the living and the dead who loved them. Their bond would transcend the veil between worlds.

Chapter 23

That afternoon, Eleri and Gareth watched as Mary and John said, 'I do.' Tears welled in Eleri's eyes and she scrubbed them away with the back of her hands. It was so beautiful. The gallery was adorned with paintings and elegant flowers. Ghosts and mortal family, all familiar faces, were upturned, rapt. At least she could fix her makeup with a thought. She sniffed. She would be forever known as the spectral panda bride at the end of this if she couldn't!

As the reception was in full swing and people danced to the music, Mary and John nodded at Eleri and Gareth, and they all slipped out.

Eleri was nervous, watching the men leave down the corridor. Mary stood by her side.

"Ready Eleri?"

Eleri swallowed, "Yes." She closed her eyes and imagined her lilac suit turning into the white gown she'd chosen with Ffion earlier. As she opened them again, she saw mist-like layers floating around her legs in an unseen breeze. In her hands, against the white heart-shaped corset, she cradled a bouquet. Orchids spilling down to her feet.

"How do I look?"

"Beautiful."

"So do you." Although Mary had changed out of her wedding dresses, she wore a beautiful wedding outfit of her own.

"Let's do this." Eleri drifted down the grand staircase of the National Library of Wales, her ivory gown trailing behind her like liquid pearl. She inhaled deeply, calming her nerves as the witching hour of midnight approached. Making her way across the marble foyer, she stepped out into the crisp night air on to the stone steps.

The air hung heavy with the cloying fragrance of night-blooming jasmine and gardenia as Eleri glided down the stone steps. Her stomach fluttered with butterflies as her hand lightly traced the cold, rough-hewn balustrade. The moon cast an eerie silvery glow across the courtyard, and the wispy willow trees sighed and creaked in a mournful midnight breeze. Strange echoes seemed to emanate from the shadowed colonnade, where wind chimes tinkled a melody.

Tiny luminescent motes drifted up from the grass, swirling around her diaphanous gown. Trellises sighed and creaked in a spectral breeze.

As Eleri reached the final step, the pungent scent of narcissus and roses clung to her senses, emanating from the bouquets adorning each vine-wrapped pillar. Their perfume seemed unnaturally strong and heady in the still night air.

A swell of nervous exhilaration bloomed inside her chest. Her heart singing as she caught sight of Gareth waiting below, as handsome as ever. She wanted to freeze this moment and live inside it forever.

When Gareth took her hand, a tingling warmth spread up her arm at his tender touch. She met his gaze, reading the devotion and adoration in his eyes, and thought her heart might burst.

As they exchanged misty rings, tears of joy pricked Eleri's eyes. She blinked them back, not wanting to cry and ruin the beautiful moment.

Eleri noticed Aunt Ffion dabbing at the corner of her eye with a spectral handkerchief. Eleri felt a surge of emotion to see her aunt so moved.

Gareth's phantom touch drew her attention like a tendril of icy vapour, raising goosebumps on her skin. A crackling energy surged across her arms, making the fine hairs stand on end.

"I can't believe this is happening," she breathed, sliding the band onto his finger.

Gareth gave her hand a gentle squeeze before releasing it to take her ring. "I've waited so long for this moment," he whispered back fervently.

The flowers nodded softly in the breeze, their waxy petals seeming to glow with an eerie luminescence in the cold moonlight. The entire world held its breath, so silent she could hear the frantic pounding of her own heart.

Her aunt stood proud with tears in her eyes, surrounded by all those who had supported her in the past year. Eleri mouthed a grateful thank you as she looked at the decorations. There was no way she could have afforded a real wedding like this. She couldn't tell what was created and what was real. John and Mary were the sole mortals destined to witness it. She couldn't have asked for a more perfect birthday, Christmas and a wedding rolled into one.

Her best friend Mary was beaming beside John under one of the phantom trellises, practically vibrating with excitement.

But it was the ghostly figure of Aunt Ffion glowing with supernatural radiance that drew Eleri's gaze, her auburn hair shimmering like copper under the twinkling lights. She gave Eleri a delighted smile.

"Dearly beloved, we are gathered here today to join this man and this woman in holy matrimony,"

As Aunt Ffion began solemnly leading them through the vows, Eleri snuck a sidelong glance at Gareth. "You look so handsome," she whispered.

Gareth met her gaze, his eyes twinkling. "And you look ravishing, cariad," he murmured back.

Ffion's voice grew thick with emotion. She collected herself, wispy trails of light drifting down her cheeks where ghostly tears fell.

"With the power vested in me by the eternal cosmos," Ffion declared fervently when the rite was complete, "I now pronounce you ghost and phantom." She beamed through her tears, her form shimmering with joy. "You may share the kiss of everlasting union."

When Aunt Ffion pronounced them married, Eleri wanted to jump and shout for joy. She settled for beaming at Gareth instead, unable to contain her euphoria. This was all she had wished for, every lonely night apart from him.

Gareth leaned in close. "Are you ready for an eternity with me, my phantom bride?" he asked, voice brimming with playful affection.

"I'm ready for forever," Eleri whispered just before their lips met in a passionate kiss. She felt Gareth smile against her mouth.

Gareth took a step back and seemed to devour her with his gaze, then swept Eleri into his arms. As their eyes locked once more, the air grew heavy with anticipation. "I love you," they uttered fervently in unison. Eleri looked up at Gareth, heart brimming. Their love stretched beyond the vanishing point, past the blurry horizon where infinity beckoned. An eternal flame that would never gutter or fade.

The moment the words left their lips, a shockwave rippled outwards, making the flowers tremble and the trellises creak. Ghostly music warped, bouncing across octaves in a haunting clash of notes. The temperature plummeted, and their breath came out in misty plumes.

Strange winds swirled through the courtyard. Eleri's veil fluttered wildly. The glowing motes that were swirling around them froze in mid-air. A humming power pressed at the edges of the courtyard, swaying the grass and rustling the leaves with unseen energy.

Eleri's bouquet glowed supernaturally bright, each luminous orchid saturated with otherworldly hues. Gareth's edges seemed to blur and glow as the mystical union took hold.

As they kissed, the electric current of their supernatural bond sang through the air with a resonant harmony that seemed to reverberate to her core.

The world held its breath, acknowledging the profound power of a love that transcended realms. Eleri and Gareth's spirits had become eternally fused, and the foundations of reality trembled in recognition.

Later, as Eleri and Gareth danced, Ffion floated over to them, still misty-eyed.

"Oh, cariad, I'm just so happy for you," she effused, fresh ghostly teardrops gliding down her cheeks. "After all this time, to see you joined in eternal love...it's all I ever wanted."

She took Eleri's hand, her touch chilling yet comforting. "Your parents would be so proud," she whispered.

Eleri hugged her aunt tight, blinking back her own joyful tears, beyond grateful to have Ffion witness her precious day. Though Ffion's form was now ghostly, her loving wisdom shone as bright as ever. With Gareth and Aunt Ffion by her side, Eleri knew their marriage would last.

The clock struck midnight. Bursts of fireworks flooded the sky above them in dazzling streams of light. Mary cheered, raising her hands in joyful blessing as her guests flooded out of the library to watch the spectacle.

Then Aunt Ffion conjured her ghostly magic. Otherworldly veils of colour merged with the fireworks, weaving hauntingly beautiful illusions.

Eleri watched the display in wonder, then back to Gareth. She had never felt so happy. This midnight wedding was pure magic.

As the fireworks faded and the echoes of cheers softened into the night, Eleri and Gareth drifted arm in arm through the courtyard under the twinkling lights. Though their feet never quite touched the ground, their hearts felt lighter than air.

"I can't believe we're finally married, cariad," Eleri said, squeezing Gareth's hand. "I've wanted this for so long."

Aunt Ffion walked up to them. "I never thought you'd break the curse. We've been willing you both to tell each other you love each other for months! Cadwgan never told Amelie he loved her. You had to both say it, and mean it."

"Was that why you kept appearing?"

"Of course. I was really panicking. None of us could tell you what the curse was about. You had to mean it. If you hadn't Gareth would have been reborn and you would have been separated forever. You were the last chance, the last descendant."

Eleri and Gareth stared into each other's eyes, startled.

"That's all it took to say I love you?" Gareth asked. "We might have said it too late."

"But we said it and I felt the curse lift." Eleri murmured.

Gareth smiled down at her, his rugged features glowing in the moonlight. "I never dreamed I'd find a love like yours, even in the afterlife. You've made eternity brighter, cariad. And happy birthday!"

Eleri laughed, surprise lighting up her face. "I can't believe I forgot my own birthday!"

They paused beneath an ivy-wrapped trellis, the occasional firework still flowering across the sky behind them. Gareth brushed a wispy curl back from Eleri's face and kissed her, soft and slow.

When they parted, Eleri glanced around the empty courtyard. "Where did Aunt Ffion and Mary go?"

"I believe they wanted to give us some privacy," Gareth chuckled. "Your aunt is likely conjuring up some other supernatural delights for the evening."

As if on cue, a haunting melody began to play, though no musicians could be seen. Ethereal notes hung on the night air like fading stars.

Gareth bowed and offered a transparent hand. "May I have this dance, Mrs Owen?"

Eleri curtsied, eyes sparkling. "I would be delighted, Mr Owen.

They moved gracefully through the courtyard in a wispy waltz, spinning weightlessly between moonbeams. Everything else fell away until only the music and each other remained.

After the courtyard had emptied following the ceremony, John and Mary made their way over to the newlywed ghosts, arm-in-arm.

"Congratulations, you two!" Mary exclaimed, beaming at her best friend. "I'm thrilled for you both."

She embraced Eleri in a brief, slightly chilling hug. As she pulled back, tears glimmered in her eyes. "I've always wanted this for you, Eleri," Mary said. "After everything...you deserve this joy."

Eleri squeezed her hand, a cool mist swirling around their entwined fingers. "Thank you, Mary. For being here, for everything." Deep friendship and gratitude shone in her gaze. "And congratulations to you and John as well on your recent nuptials."

John shook Gareth's phantom hand. "You're a lucky man, Gareth. Take good care of our Eleri, you hear?"

Gareth smiled. "I wouldn't dream of doing anything else. And you take care of Mary - she's a treasure."

Mary giggled and hugged John's arm affectionately.

"We're so pleased you could be here to share this special night with us," Eleri added, her voice brimming with gratitude.

"We wouldn't have missed it for the world," John replied sincerely.

"And just remember - you'll always be able to find us at the bakery for a chat and a cuppa. It's not every day your friends get to discover you're ghosts!"

"I'll be there for those calorie free cakes!" Mary chimed in. She rubbed her belly exaggeratedly, eliciting a chuckle from Eleri.

John let out a snort and shook his head with amusement. "Only you would get this excited about ghost cakes." He slung an arm around her shoulders.

Gareth met Eleri's twinkling gaze, a wry smile twisting his lips. "Well, this day certainly took an odd turn."

Eleri laughed, the sound bright and melodic. "That's one way of putting it."

"Mary and I've had a chat and we've decided to stay in Aber." John jerked his hand up to stall them. He grinned. "We're going to set up a travel agency in your bakery. That way, you can stay there and not be forced out by new owners. We can sell holidays and you can sell cakes at the same time. You can still stay in the flat upstairs, because we'll carry on living in

Borth.”

Eleri's hand moved to her mouth. “Oh my god, that would be lovely. Us ghosts can still snoop on the living and have a place of our own! Thank you! You'll always have free cakes with us.”

“We'd better get back to our party or my parents will wonder where we've gone. I'm so happy for you guys,” Mary said.

“Diolch Mary, for everything.”

“Hwyl, see you after the honeymoon!” With that, John and Mary went back inside.

When the song ended, they drifted to a stop beneath the tallest trellis. Eleri laid her head on Gareth's chest, listening to the silence where his heartbeat once was.

“You know, there's one thing about that newspaper article that bugs me.”

“What?”

“They got my age wrong!”

Gareth laughed, “At least they made you younger, cariad.”

Eleri tilted her face up to the inky sky as languid snowflakes drifted down. They landed feather-light in her hair, icing the dark red strands with shimmering white. She blinked as delicate flakes kissed her cheeks and eyelashes. Their icy lacework swirled through the air, dancing in the glow of the streetlamps before spiralling down to blanket the sleeping earth.

Eleri squeezed Gareth's arm, a contented sigh escaping her lips. “I wish this moment could last forever.”

Gareth tipped her chin up to meet his tender gaze. “My love, we have all eternity ahead together. And I, for one, plan to cherish every spectral moment.”

He drew her close, and they kissed once more under the moonlight.

Note from the Author

Hello, from Wales! Thank you for taking an interest in my novel. This is the part of my novel where I like to spend a few minutes to talk about the writing of this book.

You'll notice that the story is in British English, with a few Welsh words sprinkled in for good measure. It is set in my hometown of Aberystwyth, where most people I knew would speak in English but add a few Welsh words and phrases because we could, and it just felt right. I wanted to create an immersive experience from the perspective of Eleri and Gareth that would give you a flavour of the place where I grew up. At the beginning I gave a glossary of the words I used to make the story more enjoyable but you should get most of them from context.

If you spot any errors, feel free to let me know at my website CeriClark.com. You might wonder why Ceri Clark, when the author is Ceridwen Hughson. Well, they are both my real names. I was born Ceridwen Hughson and married into the Clark clan. All my fiction will be put under my Ceridwen Hughson name to separate the novels from diaries, password books, tech manuals and the like.

If you enjoyed my sweet romance novel, please leave a review where you bought this and let any friends who might like this novel know. This is a standalone novel, but I've left it open for Eleri, Gareth, Mary, and John to help other residents to find love. I have a few ideas! Don't forget to let me know if you want more of this story! I'm always happy to get helpful feedback.

Until next time,
Ceri Hughson (or Clark, I answer to both).

www.ingramcontent.com/pod-product-compliance
Lightning Source LLC
Chambersburg PA
CBHW011224190726
48287CB00008B/2743